T0158913

The Boy Who Wanted to Be a Man

A Novella

By Paul Bouchard

iUniverse, Inc.
New York   Bloomington

The Boy Who Wanted to Be a Man
A Novella

iUniverse books may be ordered through booksellers or by contacting:

iUniverse
1663 Liberty Drive
Bloomington, IN 47403
www.iuniverse.com
1-800-Authors (1-800-288-4677)

Because of the dynamic nature of the Internet, any Web addresses or links contained in this book may have changed since publication and may no longer be valid. The views expressed in this work are solely those of the author and do not necessarily reflect the views of the publisher, and the publisher hereby disclaims any responsibility for them.

The views expressed in Paul Bouchard's books are solely his own and are not affiliated with the United States army.

ISBN: 978-1-4502-2658-5 (sc)
ISBN: 978-1-4502-2660-8 (hc)
ISBN: 978-1-4502-2659-2 (ebk)

Printed in the United States of America

iUniverse rev. date: 09/27/2012

To my parents—*Mariette et Lucien*—who taught me right from wrong, the value of hard work and resourcefulness, and the importance of unconditional love.

Acknowledgments

I couldn't have written this novella without the assistance of the following people:

Mark Whitcomb, Brian Collin, and Jean Simard—their expertise on deer hunting was invaluable.

My mother, Mariette, provided some important details on the St. John Valley and northern Maine.

And finally, I am heavily indebted to Robert Barnsby and Charlie McElroy. Their sharp and critical eyes always make my manuscripts better.

Little Roger Nadeau was having dinner with his parents, Bob and Jeannette. It was a Thursday night in October of 1979, and the trio was at the dinner table in their home in Frenchville, Maine.

Bob, forty-two, was a forklift operator at Fraser Paper, a large paper mill in the adjacent town of Madawaska, while Jeannette, thirty-nine, was a seamstress at the non-union textile mill in nearby Fort Kent. Bob and Jeannette had three children: Bill, eighteen, who was in the Army and currently stationed in Panama; Lisa, thirteen, a member of the French Club and currently taking part in an 8th-grade class-sponsored trip to Quebec City, Canada; and Little Roger, eleven. Though Roger was of average height and weight for his age, "Little Roger" was his nickname nonetheless because the nickname "ti" was very common in French, and "ti" translated to "little" in English.

The Nadeaus were one of five hundred or so families who lived in Frenchville, a small town that hugged the St. John River—a river that in some parts served as the border between Maine and Canada. Nestled in the northernmost corner of the northernmost of the New England states, Frenchville was close to four hundred miles north of the port city of Portland, and some two hundred miles north of Bangor.

"And how was your day at school, Little Roger?" asked Jeannette as she took a bite of her steak.

"Good, Mommy," replied Little Roger. He took a quick sip from his glass of milk. "Pretty regular day—I've got homework and all. But I did get this interesting assignment from Mr. Morneau for our history class."

"Oh, what's that?" asked his mom, genuinely interested.

"Well, Mr. Morneau told our class that every student has to write a ten-page paper by Thanksgiving about a topic we covered in class."

"That sounds interesting," said Jeannette, a petite French Canadian brunette with rosy cheeks.

Bob, wearing his work clothes of blue jeans and a flannel shirt, chimed in with, "Yeah, sounds like you'll be busy with that assignment, Little Roger."

"Well see, Mom and Dad, that's not the half of it," Little Roger said in an excited tone. He took another quick sip of milk, and then he said, "See, after class, Mr. Morneau came up to me as I was leaving, and he said, 'Little Roger, I want your paper to be about Frenchville and the St. John Valley.' That's when I said, 'But Mr. Morneau, Frenchville and the Valley weren't covered in our history textbook,' and then he said, 'I know, Little Roger, but I'm making an exception with you. I liked your last book report about Mickey Mantle and Jackie Robinson, and I don't even like baseball. You write well about people, Little Roger. Write about the Valley, and you can also write about people and your parents."

"Well, that's a nice compliment Mr. Morneau gave you, eh, Little Roger," Bob said as he gently patted Little Roger on the shoulder. "Atta boy."

"Yes, Little Roger, congratulations," added Jeannette.

"Thank you. Thank you, Mom and Dad." Little Roger was all smiles. "But I need your help. I need help describing the Valley, and I'll need to know more about your families—my aunts and uncles."

The next fifteen minutes or so involved Little Roger asking numerous questions of his parents—questions whose answers would help him write his latest history assignment. At one point, Little Roger took a break from the Q and A because he was getting so much information, he needed to get a history-paper notebook to take notes and write it all down.

"Don't forget to mention that the Valley is basically French Canadian on both sides of the border," reminded Jeannette.

"Yes, but French is dying on the American side," added Bob, spreading margarine on a slice of white bread. "The kids still speak French, but it's dying a slow death."

Seconds later, Jeannette said, "Little Roger, I think you need to mention that Valley residents are almost all Catholics. Your dad is a Knight of Columbus, you know."

"Okay, Mommy." He wrote down *Dad—K of C.*

Suddenly, the phone rang.

"I'll get it," said Bob. He took a napkin, wiped his mouth, and went to the small foyer next to the kitchen where the phone was. "Hello."

"Mr. Nadeau?"

"Yes. Speaking."

"Mr. Nadeau, my name is Captain Richardson. I'm calling from Panama. I'm your son's company commander."

"Is there a problem?" Bob asked, genuinely concerned. He was still standing up, with the phone receiver hugging his ear.

"Well, I'm afraid your son is AWOL, sir."

Bob, not being a military man, was not following. He asked, "What does that mean, sir? What is this AWOL?"

"Stands for absent without leave, Mr. Nadeau. It means your son is absent. We haven't seen him or heard from him in over a week."

"Oh, I see," said Bob.

There was a pause and then, "Mr. Nadeau, I will keep you posted on any developments on our end, and if you learn of your son's whereabouts, please let us know."

"Yes, of course," answered Bob.

The captain gave Bob his contact information in Panama.

"Who was that?" asked Jeannette when Bob returned to the dinner table. Not one to sugarcoat things, Bob got right to the point: "That was one of Bill's military officers. He said they haven't heard from Bill in over a week."

"Is he in trouble?" asked Jeannette, her tone a worried one.

"I don't know. You know Bill—he's always been an independent sort. I'm sure he's okay."

"Maybe he's out hunting, Dad."

"Uh, I don't know, Little Roger. Sure, Bill likes to hunt, but Panama is not like here. Remember Bill's last letter? He said Panama is jungle. Not sure if there's a lot of hunting there."

The Nadeaus resumed eating. Bob, ever the optimist, always looked on the positive end of things, and though he was concerned about Bill, his concern was not overwhelming because in the end, Bill was independent and resourceful. *Bill's probably hooked up with some GIs and they're out drinking and chasing girls,* he thought. As for Jeannette, she was worried about Bill, but seeing that Bob had defused the matter some meant things couldn't be all that bad.

More passing of time at the dinner table ensued, and Bob at one point asked for seconds.

"Mommy, tell me, what was it like growing up in Clair?" Little Roger asked. His mother's hometown was in nearby New Brunswick, Canada.

"Well, Little Roger," she said, "you know I grew up on a small farm and that my father—your grandfather Long—also owned a small sawmill." Jeannette proceeded to talk about tending to large gardens in the spring and summer, shoveling snow in the winter with her siblings, helping her father with yet another side business that involved boiling maple sap in a small cabin to derive maple syrup, how Catholic Mass—when she was growing up—was all in Latin and no one knew Latin, and then, "Where I'm from, a boy is not considered a man until he kills a deer. Both my brothers—your Long uncles—killed deer before they were sixteen. Gerard killed one when he was thirteen; Maurice got his first when he was ten."

***

After dinner, Little Roger went to his bedroom to do his homework, but before he got started, he went to the small desk that occupied the north corner of his bedroom. He pulled open the desk's top drawer and removed an eight-and-a-half-by-eleven-inch notebook that was green in color.

My Goals Notebook, he thought as he looked at the notebook. He flipped open the notebook, grabbed a pen from the desk drawer, and wrote the following:

> GOAL: Get an A on history paper, Mr.
> Morneau's class.
> I want to become a man. I want to kill a deer
> and become a man.

He closed the notebook, placed it in the desk drawer, and closed the drawer. Then he started his homework for the next day's classes.

Period One—Reading. That's what Little Roger read from his homework assignment notepad, a notepad he had placed on his bed. The first entry was his first-period class, which was reading. The words *Period One—Reading* were written in his own handwriting.

Mr. Daigle assigned us fifteen pages of O Pioneers! *by Willa Cather. Boring,* thought Little Roger. *I much prefer reading about Mickey Mantle and Johnny Bench and General George Patton.* Then he paused for a second or two. *Hmm, I bet Mr. Daigle will ask us some questions about the reading tomorrow. Well, I better read those fifteen pages and get ready to answer some questions if I get called on.*

He peeked down at his assignment notepad.

Period Two—Science. Do four problems on page 83.

Darnit, thought Little Roger. *Fifteen pages of O Pioneers! and three science problems. That will take me at least an hour right there.*

He continued reading from his assignment notepad.

Period Three—History. Cool, my favorite class. We've got twelve pages to read, thought Little Roger. *We're still on President Kennedy, and our next reading's about LBJ and the Great Society. Also, I need to start an outline for my history paper on the St. John Valley.*

He glanced down at his assignment notepad some more.

Period Four—English. No homework. Thank you, thank you, Mr. Bosse.

Earlier that day, shortly after Mr. Morneau had assigned the history paper to him, Little Roger had approached and persuaded Mr. Bosse to allow him to work on his "special history paper" during Friday English classes because it was Mr. Bosse's practice to assign short writing projects to his students on Fridays, and it was also his practice on Fridays to select a student and have him or her read what they wrote during that class period.

"What's the topic of your paper?" Mr. Bosse had asked Little Roger.

"It's about the Valley," Little Roger had responded. "Mr. Morneau assigned it."

"Okay, Roger, sure," Mr. Bosse had told him. "You can work on your history paper assignment during Friday English classes, but like every student in your class, I can call on you anytime and ask you to read out loud to the class what you wrote that day."

"Yes, okay, Mr. Bosse," Little Roger had told his English teacher. "Thank you, thank you very much."

All right—no problem with period four English tomorrow, Little Roger reminded himself. *Just work on your history paper during class.*

He glanced at his assignment notepad some more.

Period Five—French; Period Six—Math; Period Seven— Physical Education.

French—no problem, he thought. *Do questions on pages 41-43. That's what Mr. Lavoie assigned for tomorrow's French class.*

Little Roger liked his French class primarily because it was easy for him. His French homework almost always consisted of the conjugation of verbs: *je, tu, ils, elles, nous, vous* ... Little Roger was fairly good at that. And this—the fact that his French homework was easy for him—explained why it was Little Roger's practice to do his French homework quickly and during the short morning homeroom period before the start of classes.

I'll do my French homework during the homeroom period, tomorrow, he thought. *As for math—yuk! Math's tough stuff,* he thought. *Four problems due tomorrow for Mr. Boucher's math class. That'll be the first assignment I do tonight, because it's the toughest subject.*

He glanced down again at his assignment notepad.

Period Seven—Physical Education with Coach Dugal. Never any homework in that class, and it's the best of all my classes, thought Little Roger. *Sports are the best—even better than history.*

Little Roger got off his bed and thought, *Better get going on that homework. Then I wanna do thirty sit-ups and thirty push-ups and then take one hundred swings with my baseball bat. After that, I'll write a bit for my history paper on the St. John Valley.*

***

By nine-fifteen that Thursday night, Little Roger had finished all his homework, save French. Of all the homework assignments he had completed, he had enjoyed reading about JFK and LBJ the most.

It'll be easy to remember where LBJ got sworn in as President, thought Little Roger when he first saw the LBJ photo in his history textbook. *It's dark and people look cramped in there. They're inside a plane—that's where LBJ got sworn in.* Then he thought: *I bet anything Mr. Morneau will ask us tomorrow where LBJ was sworn in as president. If he does, I'll raise my hand for that question.*

***

After completing his homework, Little Roger stepped out of his bedroom, walked into the kitchen, and got himself a glass of water. Unlike in nearby Madawaska, where homes were connected to a public water system, all Frenchville homes had individual water wells.

Little Roger looked up at the kitchen clock as he drank the glass of water. The clock read 9:20 P.M. Then his mother entered the kitchen.

"*Ta tout fait tes devoirs, mon ti Roger?*" she asked, questioning whether he had done his homework assignments.

"*Oui, maman,*" replied Little Roger. Then he went back to his bedroom to change into his workout clothing and work on his baseball swing.

***

After changing his clothes to sweatpants and a T-shirt, Little Roger began his nightly training regimen with sit-ups. He was in his bedroom, lying down on the carpeted floor. His feet were supported by his bed.

Little Roger exercised every night for two reasons: to be in the best shape he could be in, and to be the best baseball player he could be. The latter was the primary reason, because baseball was Little Roger's passion.

The co-captain and catcher of the Frenchville Little League baseball team, Little Roger loved baseball, and his dream was to one day be the starting catcher for the Boston Red Sox. (Yes, that dream of his was written as one of his many goals in his green Goals Notebook.) Just two weeks earlier, the Frenchville Little League team had lost the Valley Championship to their archrival, the Madawaska Red Sox. In that game, Little Roger, standing in the on-deck circle, saw his good friend Garold Dubois line out to deep centerfield for the game's final out. It was at that moment that Little Roger, ever the optimist, turned around and said for all his teammates to hear, "We'll get 'em next year, gang," but inside he thought, *Will we ever beat the Madawaska Red Sox? Who knows—maybe next year.*

Little Roger started doing the sit-ups, and when he was in the up position—the position where his elbows were touching his knees—he would glance up and admire his posters of Johnny Bench and Pete Rose, posters that were scotch-taped on an adjacent wall.

Pete Rose, the great Charlie Hustle. Hustle—that's what you've got to do, he thought as he kept doing repetitions. *Especially if you're not the biggest or most talented athlete, you have to hustle.*

After thirty sit-ups, Little Roger switched to doing push-ups—thirty of them, too. It took Little Roger slightly more than a minute to do the push-ups.

Next, Little Roger stood up and started doing toe-touches and backbends, and as he stretched he again glanced at the Bench and Rose posters.

I'm eleven years old and I'm a little over five feet tall. I weigh one-hundred-ten pounds. Will I ever develop into that great backstop like Bench? he wondered. *Well, whatever. The key is to keep hustling like Pete Rose. There's room for the little guy in baseball—also soccer, of course, but I love baseball.*

After stretching, Little Roger took five steps forward, reached in his bedroom closet, and picked up his baseball bat. He also bent down and picked up the rubber-coated donut weight next to his bat. The dense donut was the weight device used to make his bat heavier during practice swings.

Little Roger placed the bat through the weight donut. He then took four steps backward, got himself into a nice stance, and started his one hundred swings.

Shoulder to shoulder, he reminded himself as he swung the weighted bat. *Two hands on the bat at all times, hands starting near right shoulder and ending with hands near left shoulder.*

Shoulder to shoulder. That was the way Little Roger swung the bat because that's how he had learned to do it at Dr. John Winkin's two-day baseball camp the previous year. The well-respected coach of the UMAINE Black Bears college team—a team that had qualified for the College World Series numerous times—had visited the St. John Valley the previous year to conduct various mini baseball camps in area high schools. Little Roger, along with many of his buddies, had attended one of the camps, and that's how Coach Winkin had taught the baseball swing: "Two hands on the bat at all times, and remember young boys—shoulder to shoulder," was how Coach Winkin had put it. "Just like the beautiful swing of the great Hall of Famer Ted Williams—shoulder to shoulder."

***

Thirty-four, Little Roger repeated after his thirty-fourth swing. *Thirty-five, thirty-six ...*

Then again, Coach Winkin had mentioned something about a new theory of baseball hitting that had come out the previous year—the Charlie Lau method, a new baseball-hitting theory that was gaining lots of notice because of the awesome numbers the great George Brett, the third baseman for the Kansas City Royals, was putting up. Lau, a minor-league catcher with a sub-.300 lifetime batting average, was now a famed hitting instructor. The hitting technique he espoused taught one to let go of the top hand during the baseball swing.

"The Charlie Lau technique does not generate power," Coach Winkin had said last year during the two-day mini camp inside the Wisdom K-to-12 School gymnasium in nearby St. Agatha. "Hitting the ball hard makes it harder for fielders to catch the ball. I recommend all our hitters on our college squad follow the Ted Williams technique. The Charlie Lau technique is okay if you have two strikes. It's good two-strike hitting. Otherwise, two hands on the bat at all times."

Seventy-eight, seventy-nine, eighty, counted Little Roger after his eightieth swing with the bat. He was breaking into a sweat. *Twenty more swings to go.*

He turned around and took three steps backward to give himself plenty of room to take swings from the left side now. Little Roger's last twenty swings always came from the left side because he was working on becoming a switch-hitter.

Mickey Mantle was the greatest switch-hitter ever, thought Little Roger as he started swinging from the left side. On occasion he'd also remind himself, *Two hands on the bat at all times* and *shoulder to shoulder.*

***

After his workout, Little Roger picked up his pajamas and went downstairs to the basement. The Nadeau home had a finished basement complete with a full bathroom, and that's where Little Roger always took his showers. He showered, put on his pajamas, and returned to his bedroom to briefly work on his history paper. At ten o'clock sharp, Little Roger turned off his bed lamp and went to sleep.

***

Little Roger dreamed most nights. Sometimes he'd remember his dreams, but most times he'd just remember bits and pieces of them.

His dreams were mostly about sports, and he often dreamed about hitting the game-winning home run to finally beat the Madawaska Red Sox in the Valley Little League Championship Series. He also often dreamed about being the starting catcher for the Boston Red Sox.

On that Thursday night—the evening of the day he set out to kill a deer in order to become a man—Little Roger's dreams were no different except for two additions: he dreamed about things he would write about in his history paper, and he dreamed that tomorrow, a Friday, he had gone hunting after school and killed a big buck deer.

"Mommy! Mommy!" yelled Little Roger in this dream as he tried to catch his breath after running out of the woods and crossing a potato field. "Mommy! Mommy! Guess what I just did about twenty minutes ago."

"What is it, Little Roger?" asked his mother, who was cooking in the kitchen. "Dinner will be ready in thirty minutes."

"Mommy, I just killed a deer about two miles from here. I killed a deer, Mommy! A big buck!"

In this dream, Little Roger's mother's face quickly radiated a huge smile because her youngest son just accomplished a great feat.

"Wow—that's great, Little Roger! That's great news. Congratulations, dear. We'll tell your father when he arrives from work, and I'll call your aunts and uncles. That's wonderful news!"

"Yes, but I need help, Mommy—help to carry the beautiful deer out of the woods," said Little Roger in this dream of his. "I grabbed the beautiful buck by the antlers, Mommy. I placed one of my hands on the deer's side, too. The deer is dead, Mommy, but he's still warm."

"Yes, yes," Jeannette said to calm her son down.

"I grabbed the antlers, Mommy, and I dragged the deer as best as I could, but I only dragged him maybe twenty feet. He weighs a lot, Mommy."

"Wow—that must be a big deer, Little Roger," said his mother, still beaming with joy.

"Yes, Mommy, he's big. His eyes are still open, too. It's like the buck is still alive and looking at me. I feel bad I killed that big deer, Mommy, but I'm a man now."

"Yes, yes you are, Little Roger. All our relatives will be proud of you. You'll be the talk of the town."

That was one of Little Roger's dreams that Thursday night— the feat of killing a deer and becoming a man. It was a new dream for him.

And then there was another new dream for Little Roger— actually, it was a series of dreams, all of which dealt with his new history-paper assignment. In his dreams, Little Roger imagined himself researching his paper, writing it, and reading it to the class, the words from his dinner-table interview with his parents still echoing in his head ...

... Clair, New Brunswick, Canada, will be easy to write about in my history paper because my Mommy's parents—my Mémère and Pépère Long—are still alive and living there.

The Longs were from the Gaspe region of Quebec, Canada, and like many of the people of the Gaspe region, they were fishermen and farmers. Pépère's father—my great grandfather—set out with another man to find available land to the south, in the province of New Brunswick.

The other man—I forget his name—then my great grandfather Long, and then Pépère Long, who was five years old at the time so the year had to be 1907 because I know Pépère Long was born in 1902—those three individuals took a train in Gaspe, Quebec, a train that was heading south. Armed with only their clothes, two axes, and hunting rifles, the two men and the five-year-old boy got off the train during one of its stops. The two men, but not the boy, knew they were in another province. They also knew that the Canadian Government in Ottawa had enacted homestead policies to help settle vast tracks of land, and that was good because it was land these two men and the boy (my grandfather) had come for, and land is what they received. All that was needed was for one to make his claim. That's what the two men did: they found nice land around present-day Clair in the province of New Brunswick and they claimed it. The claimed land had plenty of forests, hills, and rivers. The two men and the small five-year-old boy began clearing this land by chopping down trees.

The three individuals stayed for only a short time on that first trip south to New Brunswick, but the following year the same two men brought their entire families with them to the new land they claimed. These first settlers were joined by another Gaspe family—the Roys. That explains why Pépère

Long twelve years later married one of the Roy girls, Denise, who is my grandmother now.

George Long—Pépère—and Mémère had four children, two boys and two girls. Jeannette, my mother, is the last of those four children.

My mom's family speaks almost exclusively in French. Mémère and Pépère can write, and they read a little bit, even though both of them never went beyond the third grade in school. They can't speak English. Only my mom and Uncle Gerard can speak English.

Pépère was and still is a lumberjack, a hunter, a fisherman, a trapper, and a maple-syrup maker. I've noticed he's slowed down in the last couple of years, but he still does all those things. Plus he also tends a large garden where he grows all kinds of vegetables and strawberries and raspberries and rhubarb.

Boy, I love to visit my maternal grandparents in Clair. We usually visit them once a month because Pépère and Mémère live only thirty minutes from Frenchville.

Pépère and Mémère's house is painted white with green trim. It's a two-story home with small rooms. The front exterior of the home is encircled by a covered wraparound porch, the floor of which is painted bright gray. Mommy told me Pépère makes sure the porch floor is painted every three years.

I'm always impressed with the big rack of caribou antlers that hangs on the front side of my grandparents' home. Most of the time, whenever we visit my grandparents, I sit next to Pépère on the porch. We're both rocking in rocking chairs on the porch, and that's when I ask him about the big rack of antlers.

"I shot a caribou in the province of Quebec," Pépère tells me whenever I ask him this question. Of course, he tells me this

in French, and I ask him in French too because Pépère doesn't speak English.

"Big animal, that caribou," Pépère *always tells me.* "Good meat, too—not as good as deer, but still good."

On visits to my grandparents, I always make it a point to ask Pépère about his latest fur trappings, and when I do, Pépère *goes upstairs in his house, and in five minutes or so he returns downstairs to show everyone his latest beaver and fox furs.* Pépère *still traps, though not as much as before.*

A great treat during our visits to my grandparents is eating Pépère's maple-syrup products, mostly maple-sugar candies and maple-sugar cones filled with ice cream. I know Pépère—and now Uncle Gerard's sons, because they help Pépère out—has one of the best maple-syrup camps in all of New Brunswick. And last year, I learned that the Canadian government was planning on subsidizing the maple-syrup business and aggressively pursuing exports of maple-syrup products from the Clair region.

"The federal government plans to announce Clair as the maple-syrup capital of the country, Bob," Uncle Gerard told Dad in French during our last visit to Mémère and Pépère's house. I was listening attentively. "The government plans to pump a lot of money into the industry."

"That's what makes Canada different from the United States," my dad told Uncle Gerard. "Canada subsidizes business while our government does not, but I think that's why our economy is better in the long run."

"Maybe so," Uncle Gerard told Dad. "As for the maple-syrup business, we're doing okay with it. It's seasonal work, as you know, Bob. It's not enough for us to live on."

"Yes, I understand that," my dad told him.

"Right now, Bob, our big problem with maple syrup is bears. You know two years back, we switched from the old metal-bucket system to the new plastic pipe system. No more hollow nails supporting buckets filled with sap; no more walking around from maple tree to maple tree lugging heavy sap-filled buckets back to our camp to start the boiling process. Now, every tree is plugged to a plastic pipe that goes straight to the cabin. Problem is, the bears chew through the rubber coating and the plastic to get at the sap."

I love those trips to my grandparents in Clair. Boy, that caribou rack, those antlers ... that makes me think of me killing a deer and becoming a man! I hope to kill a deer tomorrow or Saturday so I can become a man!

Mémère's cooking is so good—that's one of the many things I like about our trips to my grandparents. Mémère, she cooks this meat dish called si pate which includes something like five different meats. And Mémère's tourtieres—her meat pies—boy those are good.

On these trips I especially like to observe Pépère, because he's a true pioneer. Pépère hunts, he fishes, he traps beaver and foxes, he's a lumberjack, he tends to a huge garden, and he's also a good violin player. I especially like it when Pépère taps his feet on the floor in rhythm with his violin playing.

Pépère is seventy-seven years old, and he looks great. I'm guessing he's around five feet nine inches tall, and he's slim, but he's got that solid build to him. His hair is still very thick and gray, but it's a very dark gray, not white gray at all. Pépère definitely has worker's hands—thick and creased hands from all the hard work he does. I also know that Pépère is missing two toes because of frostbite during those long cold winters of being a lumberjack. I guess the amputations were necessary.

Pépère smokes a pipe, too, and boy that pipe tobacco smells so good. Pépère smells like tobacco, but it's good-smelling tobacco—unlike Dad's cigar smoke, which sometimes gives me a headache. Pépère *likes George Washington tobacco in his pipe, and it sure does smell good.*

I've noticed that Pépère *uses these big wooden matches to light up his pipe—not the cardboard matches that Dad uses to light up his cigars, but nice thick wooden matches.* Pépère *always has long nails on his fingers. I've noticed that, too. And what he does to get his matches to light up is grab them in a certain way—all done with one hand—and, with the stroke of a thick fingernail, he flicks off the head of the match. With the match burning, he inhales from his pipe that's stuffed with George Washington tobacco, and then he lights up the tobacco. I'm always amazed at that: holding a match in one hand and using a fingernail from the same hand, flicking off once, maybe twice, at the head of the match and creating a flame.*

Pépère *is good around animals, too. He knows animals, and he knows their ways, and he isn't afraid of any animal.*

Pépère *and* Mémère *have a nice dog in their home, a black mutt who has a lot of Doberman pinscher in him. He's a good and obedient dog and always obeys* Pépère's *commands.*

My family, we have a nice little Chihuahua named Dino. Dino always sleeps with Mommy. Dino, like most Chihuahuas, is a nervous and aggressive little dog. Chihuahuas are okay around people they know, but strangers are a different story.

I'll never forget how Pépère *handled Dino's first visit to* Pépère's *house.* Pépère *was in his rocking chair on the porch and I was in an adjacent rocking chair. Little Dino was walking about, sniffing at the porch floor, checking out a home he'd never been in. When Little Dino got close to* Pépère's *chair,* Pépère *said in French, "That's a nice little dog," and proceeded to attempt to hold and pet Dino.*

I saw disaster coming because I knew Dino was aggressive, that he would bite people he didn't know. And this time would be no different because as soon as Pépère picked up Dino, Dino started biting and biting and biting some more, struggling to get Pépère to let him go.

I was so amazed. For one thing, Pépère withstood all those bites and Dino's vigorous struggle to get free. And then, maybe after ten seconds of biting, Dino calmed down for a while. After a few more seconds passed, Dino was comfortable enough to let Pépère hold him and pet him at will. Pépère is incredible around animals.

Mémère—she's stocky and heavy-set. She's a great cook, too. Unfortunately, Mémère has diabetes, but she looks strong at seventy-five years old.

Mommy's sisters and brothers—my aunts and uncles on Mom's side of the family—are all nice people. My two Long uncles worked in the iron-ore mines of Schefferville, Quebec, at one time, but then those mines shut down. Uncle Gerard, he runs a Christmas-tree farm along with the maple-syrup camp. He's married and has two children, and he lives next to Pépère and Mémère in Clair. I also know my Uncle Gerard hunts and fishes a lot, and he does carpentry work, too. Last year Uncle Gerard told Dad, "I receive an unemployment check—in French we call it a chomage cheque—for half the year."

Uncle Maurice, my other Long uncle, works for Fraser Paper at their mill in Edmunston, New Brunswick. He and his wife, Pauline, have three children. Uncle Maurice also hunts and fishes. Oh, and both Uncle Maurice and Uncle Gerard smoke Players cigarettes, drink plenty of LaBatts beer, and they like to play cards.

Aunt Loraine, Mommy's sister, is a very nice woman. She's a homemaker and lives with her husband, Claude, in Clair, New Brunswick. They have two children. I know for a fact that my Aunt Loraine is a renowned cook because she's always asked to cook whenever there are big weddings or big church functions. I also know that when the archbishop of the diocese visited the parish in Edmunston, it was my aunt, Loraine Levesque, who was asked to be in charge of all meals for the bishop and visiting party.

From my mom, I really feel my French Canadian roots. Gosh, it was just last year when I learned from Mommy that Canadians are mostly English speakers. Here in northern Maine, we're close to both Quebec and the French-speaking part of New Brunswick. Pierre Trudeau speaks both French and English, and I thought that's how most Canadians were— you know, bilingual. But Mommy told me last year that except for Quebec and some parts of New Brunswick, Canada is all English-speaking.

Me, I think borders matter. Even if the Valley is both American and Canadian and there are similar things about the people on both sides of the border, I think there are a lot of differences, too. The currency is different—that's one example. Prices are also different for some things, too. Cigarettes and beer are very expensive in Canada. That's why there's a big illegal smuggling trade in those products between Maine and New Brunswick. Plus, the drinking age in Quebec is eighteen; it's nineteen in New Brunswick. Here in Maine, the legal drinking age is twenty-one. Also, here in Maine we start school at five years old, but in Canada they start at six. Mommy told me Canadians graduate from high school at the age of nineteen, and college is basically free for public universities, while here in the United States we have to pay for college. Sports are another subject where I see differences. My cousins, like Andre and Jules, they play hockey. Hockey is big in Canada. Here in Frenchville, we just have pick-up hockey games, but we don't have organized hockey like they do in Canada. And here in Maine we play baseball and also basketball.

Mommy also told me that healthcare is free in Canada, but the waiting lines to see a doctor are long. And Mommy also told me taxes are very high in Canada because someone has to pay for all those free things like education and health care and "paying those chomage checks."

Also, Mommy once told me that military service is not a big thing in Canada like the military is here in the United States.

"If your brother Bill were Canadian, he probably wouldn't be in the Canadian Army. He probably wouldn't have chosen to enlist in the military. Now look at him ... poor Bill, lost in some place in Panama."

My dad, like Mommy, also has an interesting family history. He's the third of four children.

My dad's parents, Mémère and Pépère Nadeau, grew up in Frenchville. I never saw my Nadeau grandparents because they both died before I was born. My mémère Nadeau died while she was giving birth, and the child also died. What I do know was that Mémère Nadeau was a hard-working woman who was a homemaker and a businesswoman. Dad told me she operated a small hot-dog stand in the summer months, and apparently she made good money with it.

Pépère Nadeau, he worked for a potato farmer in Frenchville. He also owned and farmed forty acres of potatoes. Dad told me his father died of a heart attack two years after Mémère had died.

According to dad, his parents were well-respected in Frenchville—the Nadeaus were always known to be hard workers and honest. Dad also told me his parents were always trying to get ahead in life—always working hard and trying to start little businesses like selling Christmas trees, selling fashionable hats for women, selling milk, and selling hot dogs, too.

"My parents worked hard, very hard," Dad told me once. "My mother was a good businesswoman. Her hot-dog stand worked well, but all the other small businesses were money losers."

Dad has a brother and two sisters. Uncle Gilles, like Dad, works at Fraser Paper in Madawaska. Uncle Gilles likes hunting, fishing, and snowmobiling. He also fixes old cars, and he has a motorcycle. Uncle Gilles and his wife, Suzanne, have three children. They live in Madawaska.

Aunt Claudette, Dad's sister, is a hairdresser in Bangor, Maine. We don't see her too often except for the holidays because Bangor is almost four hours from Frenchville. Boy, I would love to play baseball someday for the University of Maine Black Bears in Orono, Maine. Orono is real close to Bangor—just like Madawaska is close to Frenchville. Playing college baseball and seeing Aunt Claudette more often would be good.

My dad's other sister is Aunt Isabelle. She married a Canadian man. They own a restaurant outside Montreal now. We went to Montreal two years ago and visited them. Dad said Montreal was six hours away from Frenchville. Our trip was in the late fall and baseball was over. I would have loved to see the Expos play in Olympic Stadium. It's funny how you remember things: I know that trip to Montreal was two years ago, in 1977, because I wanted to visit Montreal and Aunt Isabelle in 1976 when Montreal was hosting the Olympics. That's when Dad said the traffic was too crazy in Montreal. "Driving and parking will be impossible, Little Roger," he told me. "We'll go next year." We did.

Little Roger suddenly woke up. He was very comfortable in his bed, but he was also very thirsty, so he decided to get up, go to the kitchen, and get himself a glass of water.

As he drank the water, Little Roger glanced up at the kitchen clock to check the time. The clock read 1:10 A.M.

Little Roger knew he had just been dreaming, but he couldn't remember much about his dream. When he returned to bed, he forced himself to think about the things he had just dreamed about. He knew there was something about *Pépère* Long in his rocking chair smoking his pipe and smelling good because the tobacco he was smoking smelled good. This *Pépère* Long image also had Dino in it—*Pépère* Long was petting little Dino. Then there was the image of his grandmother Nadeau selling hot dogs. That was the other image Little Roger could remember about his latest dream.

Little Roger got back in his bed, but he couldn't fall asleep. As he lay in his warm bed, he glanced at both his Pete Rose and Johnny Bench posters. He also thought about Pépère Long.

Pépère probably killed a deer when he was just a little boy—maybe seven years old or something like that.

A few minutes passed. Little Roger still couldn't fall asleep even though he was comfortable in his bed. That's when he decided to pray the following: *Dear Lord, I'm not sure if this is an okay subject to pray for. I know we're supposed to pray to ask for forgiveness of our sins, and I know we're supposed to be thankful for the many things we have, but dear Lord, I really want to be a man. I want that, and I'm sorry if I have to kill one of the beautiful animals you created. If killing a deer is a sin, dear Lord, then I am sorry for the sin I might commit. Please understand, Lord, that I will only kill one deer, and I will only do this once, this one time. Amen.*

Fifteen minutes later, Little Roger fell asleep, and ten minutes after that, unbeknownst to him, he started dreaming again.

Little Roger started dreaming about playing baseball for the UMAINE Black Bears and then getting drafted by the Boston

Red Sox. He also dreamed about hitting a home run to beat the Madawaska Red Sox in next year's Little League Valley Championship. And then his dream suddenly shifted—it shifted to him killing a big buck deer and seeing the joy on his mother's face because of his recent accomplishment of becoming a man. A flash image of that dream included Little Roger surrounded by his relatives at a dinner table. The day was Sunday, two days after Little Roger's great feat of killing a deer and leaping into manhood. His mom was serving cake and ice cream. His dad and Uncle Gilles, both Americans, were drinking Schlitz and smoking King Edward cigars, while his Canadian uncles, Gerard and Maurice, were drinking Labatt's Blue and puffing on Players cigarettes. A card game was about to break out, and then *Pépère* Long, who was smoking his pipe, stood up erect and said in French, "Congratulations to our Little Roger for killing a one-hundred-eighty-pound buck on Friday. He is no longer a boy. Our Little Roger is a man." And then *Pépère* Long raised a glass of Labatt's Blue beer and said, "To Little Roger. Eleven years old and a man!" Everyone with a glass toasted one another.

And then Little Roger's dream shifted again, this time to the history paper he had to write and ...

There's quite a few World War II veterans from Frenchville.

I still remember the time when the St. John Valley Times *ran a great article on Claude Morneau and how he helped save his American GI buddies in North Africa.*

Claude was stationed in North Africa to fight Rommel's troops. The Desert Fox supposedly was a brilliant general—I hate recognizing the Nazis, but everything I've read says he was a great general. Well, Claude Morneau, who is actually Mr. David Morneau's uncle, was captured by the Germans along with some of his American GI buddies from his unit. These

American soldiers were held as prisoners by the Germans, but it was Claude who led and managed their escape, all because he spoke French and got local French-speaking Muslims to help him and his buddies escape from the Germans.

I remember reading how a St. John Valley Times reporter got hold of the story about this escape. A fellow war buddy of Claude's—a guy from upstate New York—came to Frenchville to visit Claude a couple years ago. Word of this man's visit spread around Frenchville, and then the local newspaper editor assigned a reporter to write the story about how the American soldiers escaped their German captors a long time ago in North Africa. I really should mention Claude's heroic efforts in my history paper—it's a great story, and it'll probably give me some brownie points with Mr. Morneau, my history teacher, who's the nephew of Claude.

Which reminds me ... the Morneaus are all nice people. Mommy told me that Mrs. Morneau, David Morneau's grandmother, had twenty kids. Twenty kids! Actually, there's an Albert family in St. Agatha that also has twenty kids, and I know Mommy once told me there's a Levesque family across the river in St. Hillaire, Canada, with twenty-four children. I should mention this too in my history paper, how some Valley families are very big. I think that's because we're all Catholic. I'll ask Mommy about that.

Mommy also told me that Mrs. Morneau had seven of her sons fighting in World War II all at the same time—seven! Claude was in Africa. One of his brothers was in Burma. Most of the Morneau boys were fighting on the European front, but some were stationed in Asia, too. Seven brothers fighting in World War II—that's the Morneaus for you.

My dad, he never joined the military, but I know he was happy when Bill joined the Army. Dear Lord, please have Bill call us from Panama. I don't know what AWOL is—I heard

Mommy say she too didn't know what AWOL is. Anyway, Bill is missing. I know he's okay because he knows how to live in the woods. Lord, please have Bill call us.

Little Roger then dreamed about Panama. The images made Little Roger think of Florida—*what was it about Florida?*

Hmm … Florida? Oh yes, Florida. Dad told me when he was a truck driver in Connecticut, he took three weeks off and went down to Florida with some friends. Dad told me they made it all the way down to Key West, Florida, and that they saw the house of Ernest Hemingway. I know Ernest Hemingway because his photo is in our history textbook for Mr. Morneau's class. His photo was next to President Kennedy's photo.

And then Little Roger dreamed about his dad drinking beer with Ernest Hemingway and President Kennedy. His dad, Ernest Hemingway, and President Kennedy were also smoking cigars.

Then Little Roger's dream quickly shifted, this time to him and his brother Bill hunting rabbits, but the trees—the woods—they looked different, very different. That's when Little Roger realized, subconsciously, that his dream was taking place in Panama: he and Bill were hunting rabbits in the jungle of Panama, where the trees were palm trees and not the common fir and hardwood trees of Northern Maine. At one point in this dream, Little Roger spotted a rabbit. He pointed at the rabbit so Bill could see it and shoot it. It was easy for Little Roger to spot the rabbit because it had already changed to its white fur because it was in the late fall, even though the Panamanian jungle was hot and humid. Bill fired at the rabbit, and the rabbit stopped moving. Then Little Roger heard some noise, but he couldn't figure it out. He couldn't figure out the noise. He kept thinking: what is the rabbit doing? The answer wasn't coming to him. Then off to Little Roger's right, up on a hill, was his dad, Ernest Hemingway, and President Kennedy, all smoking cigars.

His dad said, "At-ah boy, Bill. Nice shot. I knew you weren't AWOL for too long—you were just hunting for a few days here in Panama." And then Little Roger's dream shifted again, this time to him killing a big buck deer ...

Little Roger with his 16-gauge shotgun ...

A slug in the shotgun's single barrel ...

Little Roger shooting the buck deer ...

Little Roger actually seeing the dark eyes of the big deer ...

It's like the deer is still alive, God—the buck deer is still looking at me even though I shot him, even though the deer is dead.

In the dream, Little Roger started running down the hill. His heart was pounding fast. He was excited of course, and he couldn't wait to tell his parents about his great achievement of killing a deer, of becoming a man.

But as he was running down the hill and about to cross a harvested potato field, the thought of the deer's eyes bothered him.

Can the deer still be alive?

Hmm?

The last time I saw eyes like that was when Mr. Voisine killed a big bull moose. The bull moose was hanging from a crane, and neighbors had gathered around Mr. Voisine's front lawn to see the huge moose hanging from the crane. Mommy and Daddy took me and Lisa to see the big moose, and I remember noticing the moose's dark brown eyes still being open. It was like the moose was still alive, like looking directly at me and saying, "Why did Mr. Voisine shoot me? I'm alive. Now get me off this crane."

"Can the deer I just shot still be alive? I better check," and so Little Roger turned around and now starts running up the hill to check if ...

Little Roger suddenly heard a knock on his bedroom door. It woke him up.

"*Reveille toi, Ti Roger,*" he heard his Mom say. "Time to get up."

Little Roger rubbed his eyes and slowly got out of bed. His mom had left the door ajar. Little Roger sneaked a peak at the kitchen clock. It read 6:20 A.M.

***

As Little Roger was getting out of bed, he immediately realized he had been dreaming, but about what? He remembered so little. He thought hard, but all he could come up with were images of his dad drinking beer with Ernest Hemingway and President Kennedy; his *Pépère* Long smoking the pipe and playing the violin; and him and his brother, Bill, hunting rabbits.

Little Roger yawned. He then went downstairs to the finished basement portion of his parents' home. He entered the basement bathroom and urinated. Next, he turned on the faucet and splashed some cold water on his face. He toweled off his wet face, and then he started brushing his teeth.

I hear footsteps, he thought as he was brushing his teeth. He quickly rinsed his mouth, and then he stepped outside the bathroom to see who was coming.

It was his dad. Little Roger saw his dad halfway down the basement stairs. Bob Nadeau was wearing his typical work attire: green work pants and green shirt, tan steel-toe boots, a John Deere cap on the top of his jet-black hair, dark sunglasses covering his eyes. His dad was also chewing on a King Edward cigar.

"Little Roger," Bob Nadeau said to his youngest son. "It's a cold morning. Go and put some wood in the furnace, please."

"Yes, Dad," replied Little Roger.

Little Roger entered the furnace room, which was next to the basement bathroom and his father's workshop. The large cement-floor furnace room was where the Nadeaus kept a cord of split wood to feed the home's furnace. It was also the room where Little Roger had his weight bench, and it's the room where he sometimes practiced his baseball swing, though he mostly did that in his bedroom.

Little Roger started loading his arms with pieces of sliced wood.

Gosh darn, he thought. *This cement floor sure is cold when you're barefoot.*

He proceeded to place the sliced wood pieces in the furnace one piece at a time. He repeated this process three times, with three loads of wood, placing wood in the furnace piece by piece. He did this hurriedly because he had a school bus to catch in about twenty minutes. He quickly shut the furnace door and exited the furnace room once he was done with his chore.

Sure feels better walking on carpet than on cement, he thought as he walked out of the furnace room and headed toward the basement bathroom. The thought prompted him to lift his left foot and turn it in such a way that he was able to see its sole.

"Darnit," he said out loud. He had suspected this. *The bottoms of my feet are all dirty from standing barefoot on the cement floor of the furnace room. What am I going to do now?* He thought quickly. *Guess I better take a quick shower and wash my feet.*

He entered the bathroom again, stripped down, and quickly hopped in the shower. Minutes later, he toweled himself off and put on his pajamas again. He then headed upstairs.

As he walked through the kitchen to get to his bedroom, Little Roger quickly glanced at the kitchen clock. The time read 6:45. He thought, *Fifteen minutes till the bus arrives.* Just then, he saw his mother in the hallway. She was dressed for work, holding a cup of coffee, and walking in his direction.

"Have a good day, *Ti Roger*," said his mother as she walked by him. She often called her youngest son *Ti Roger*, the French equivalent of Little Roger. "And why are your peejays all dirty?"

"Well, Mommy, I had to load up the furnace with wood this morning," responded Little Roger, his voice exhibiting a slight worried tone.

"I'm constantly doing wash here," said his mother as she suddenly stopped walking. She took a quick sip of coffee. "You should have worked with that split wood while wearing a work shirt or something else—at least not your peejays."

"Yes, Mommy," replied Little Roger.

"Well, your sister called last night," she said. "She's fine in Quebec City with her French Club friends. Their bus arrives tomorrow at four in the afternoon at the Wisdom School."

"That's nice," said Little Roger.

"And Dino is okay. He's in the washroom with his food and water. Oh, please make sure Dino has fresh water in his bowl."

"Yes, Mommy."

"And lock the front door, *Ti Roger*. I'll be back from my shift at the textile mill around four, and I'll fix you and your father a nice dinner tonight. How does haddock, potatoes, fresh bread, and salad sound?"

"Great, Mommy," replied Little Roger. Like many Catholics, the Nadeaus always ate fish on Fridays.

Little Roger's mother placed her empty coffee cup in the kitchen sink. She turned and walked through both the kitchen and the small office space of the home, and then she opened the door to the left—the door leading to the garage. She entered the garage, got into the black Buick family car, and drove off to work.

Little Roger glanced at the kitchen clock again. It read 6:50 A.M.

Boy, I'm running late, he reminded himself. *I better hurry to make sure I catch the bus.*

He quickly walked to the small laundry room next to the kitchen.

"*Allo, mon ti Dino,*" Little Roger said as soon as he entered the laundry room. Dino, the family dog, was a white Chihuahua with light brown patches. Comfortably lying in his dog basket, Dino started wagging his tail as soon as he saw Little Roger approach him.

Little Roger picked up Dino's water bowl and placed it under the laundry room's deep sink that was next to the washer and dryer. He poured out the old water and replaced it with new water straight from the tap. Dino was still wagging his tail, and his ears were now bent down too—signs that the little dog was happy and thankful.

Little Roger placed the water bowl in front of Dino.

"Okay, *mon ti Dino,*" he told the dog. "I'll see you later this afternoon right before I go hunting." Just as he said that, Dino rolled over on his back. Little Roger knew what this meant: Dino wanted his belly tickled.

"Okay, okay," he told Dino. "I'll pet you and tickle you, but not for long."

Little Roger bent down on one knee and gently started tickling Dino's belly. He noticed Dino's ears were bent down, and that Dino's tail was wagging even faster.

"You like that, eh, *mon ti Dino,*" he told the dog. He tickled Dino some more, and then he said, "Okay Dino, I gotta go now."

Little Roger got up and exited the laundry room, making sure he shut the door behind him so Dino wouldn't run around the house. He then went to his bedroom to quickly change clothes.

Boy, I'm running late. Don't want to miss the bus, he reminded himself as he entered his bedroom.

He hurriedly got out of his peejays and slipped into his jeans. He put on a white T-shirt, then a long sleeve blue shirt, and then he pulled white socks over his feet.

I don't want to miss the school bus.

Little Roger made sure all his books and notebooks were in his school bag. He then went to his closet to get his jacket and Nike sneakers.

Where the heck are my sneakers? he asked himself. His Nike sneakers weren't in his bedroom closet. He felt himself getting nervous. *Gosh darn, I need my sneakers.*

Frantic, Little Roger started looking everywhere in his bedroom for his Nike sneakers. He checked his closet again— twice in fact, but his sneakers weren't there. Then he got down and looked under his bed. He saw his shotgun and shells, but no sneakers.

I can't wait to go deer hunting after school, but where the heck are my sneakers? Dear God, help me.

Suddenly, a thought hit him—*Dino. Maybe Dino took them, because sometimes Dino has the habit of trotting about with shoes in his mouth. But where could Dino have put my sneakers?*

Little Roger left his bedroom in a panic.

It had to be Dino, but where could Dino have left my sneakers?

He entered the kitchen and looked at the kitchen floor. He looked and looked and ... there, directly underneath one of the kitchen-table chairs, was one of his sneakers.

Little Roger quickly put on and laced up this one sneaker. It was his left sneaker.

Well, I'm halfway there, he thought.

He started walking around the kitchen in a frantic search for his right sneaker.

Maybe Dino dragged my other sneaker to the laundry room, he thought after about fifteen seconds of frantic searching. He decided to check his latest thought.

Little Roger entered the laundry room. Dino, at first, was quietly sitting in his dog basket, but then he started wagging his tail again.

"Where's my other sneaker, Dino?" asked Little Roger out loud.

Dino continued to wag his tail. His ears were bent down again.

Little Roger scanned the washroom. He looked closely at the floor. Nothing. He looked at the space between the washer and dryer. No sneaker there either. He then decided to look inside the closet behind Dino's dog basket.

Bingo. There it was: a Nike sneaker in the middle of the closet floor.

"Bad dog, Dino. Bad dog," Little Roger said out loud. Dino started wagging his tail faster.

Little Roger quickly put on his second sneaker and laced it up. He turned around and started heading out of the laundry room when …

"Oh no!" he yelled as his left foot accidentally struck Dino's water bowl. He noticed lots of spilled water on the floor. Dino started barking loudly.

"Gosh darn, Dino, I'm running late as it is," he said, frustrated. Just as he said those words, Dino jumped out of his basket and started barking even louder.

"Okay, okay, okay, I'll fix it," said Little Roger. "I'll clean up this mess and get you new water." Dino quieted down and stopped barking.

Little Roger quickly got a towel, bent down, and started soaking up the spilled water. At one point, he instinctively looked through both the hallway and the kitchen window, all in an effort to keep an eye out for his school bus.

Oh no! The bus! The bus! he told himself when he saw the yellow school bus across the driveway. His heart started pounding. *The bus is here!*

In a panic, he filled Dino's water bowl and placed it next to Dino's basket. Dino, now barking again because of Little Roger's fast movements, suddenly started turning round and round, trying to catch the end of his tail.

"Stop that, Dino, stop it," yelled Little Roger in the hopes of bringing control to the chaos. "You can't catch your tail, Dino."

Dino, after a few seconds, stopped barking and chasing his own tail, and that's when Little Roger closed the laundry room door and raced over to his bedroom to get his jacket and book bag. He retrieved both items, raced out of his bedroom, dashed through the kitchen, and ran out the front door.

Gosh darnit—I missed my bus, he realized as he saw the back of the bus already passing the neighbor's home, the Gagnon's. He shook his head in frustration.

Little Roger turned and made sure the front door was locked behind him. He started thinking about his options, and as he did he realized it was quite chilly out. When he exhaled, his breath turned into a thin white mist. He also saw a thin frost covering the front lawn.

I'm sure it'll warm up later this morning and during the afternoon, he thought. *At least I hope so, because I don't want it to be too cold for my hunting later today.*

He pondered his options. *Call Dad at Fraser Paper? Nah, that'll take away from Dad's work. Besides, Madawaska's a long drive. Call Mommy at the textile mill? No way—Fort Kent's even farther than Madawaska. Plus I don't even know the phone number to the textile mill.*

Then a thought hit him: *I'll hitchhike to school. Yeah, hitchhiking's really the only way.*

Bob and Jeannette Nadeau knew Little Roger occasionally hitchhiked with his friends, especially in the summer months to go see men's softball games in Madawaska. Their guidance on the subject was, "Don't do it at night, and don't do it alone."

Little Roger started walking down the asphalt driveway, and as he did he prayed the following: *Forgive me, Lord. I know I'm not supposed to hitchhike alone, but I really have no choice this morning. I hope you understand. I also hope I'll see a deer today when I go hunting after school. Help me, Lord. Help me become a man.*

He crossed U.S. Route 1 and started hoping some vehicle— any vehicle heading east— would give him a ride. His hands were cold, so he placed them in his front pockets for warmth.

Well, there was the wood-in-the-furnace chore I had to do, and then I was missing my sneakers for awhile, he thought, reliving how it came that he had missed his bus. *Oh, and then I spilled Dino's water. But there was something else ... something ...*

Then he remembered: Normally the bus driver, Jim Blanchette, waited a short time when a student wasn't outside waiting for the bus. But Mr. Blanchette had no way of seeing Little Roger this morning. And besides, Lisa was usually with him waiting for the bus, but Lisa wasn't with him that morning because she was in Quebec City with the French Club students, so Mr. Blanchette probably waited some time, but when he saw no one he must have figured they were either already at school or not coming to school.

Five minutes passed and still no vehicle. Then Little Roger saw two cars, but the cars were heading toward Fort Kent, the opposite direction from where he needed to go. Still a bit cold, he started pacing around in the hopes of warming up. His book bag was strapped to his back and supported by his shoulders.

Suddenly, Little Roger saw a pickup truck out in the distance near Leonard Dufour's small gas station. He quickly recognized the pickup, a beat-up old red Dodge with a white top. Little Roger instantly smiled with relief as the pickup slowly kept coming in Little Roger's direction. When the Dodge pickup reached Richard Blanchette's nearby home, Little Roger confidently stuck out his right arm and right-hand thumb.

You know, this is really good luck, he thought. *I hope I get more of this good luck this afternoon when I'm out deer hunting.*

The fact was, Little Roger didn't only feel lucky because a vehicle was finally in sight and heading in his direction—he was happy about that, of course—but what he was really thrilled about was who owned and drove that vehicle, that old Dodge pickup heading his way.

"You must have missed your bus, huh, Little Roger?" asked the pickup's driver after he stopped his truck and Little Roger hopped in.

"Yes, Mr. Bellefleur," said Little Roger. "I'm afraid I missed my bus this morning."

Guy Bellefleur was a French Canadian—he was actually a dual citizen, American and Canadian—who had married a woman from Frenchville. For a time, the couple lived in the province of Quebec, but back in the fall of 1979 the couple's home was in Frenchville where Mr. Bellefleur, age forty-four, owned and operated a small construction business. It was widely known in Frenchville and the Valley that when Guy Bellefleur wasn't doing carpentry work, he was either fishing or hunting. And it was also widely known that last year, in 1978, Mr. Bellefleur had killed a big bull moose out by Square Lake, a sizeable lake located forty-five minutes south of Frenchville. Soon after this big kill, Bellefleur's huge dead moose was hanging from a large pulley system at Philip Dionne's Meat and Fish Market Store in Frenchville, and it was then and there that Little Roger, Lisa, Little Roger's parents, and also a few locals gathered to see the huge dead animal.

"Did you just stay in the woods hoping to see a moose?" Jeannette Nadeau had asked Mr. Bellefleur, who was standing next to his hanging dead moose and fielding questions.

"No, Jeannette, the female moose makes a horn sound that attracts the bull to her," he had replied. "I just did the best I could to make that sound. In twenty-five minutes, I saw the bull moose heading in my direction."

***

"Well I guess you got up late and that's why you missed your bus, heh?" asked Mr. Bellefleur as his right foot pressed on the throttle to pick up some speed.

"Ah, well, actually, I had a few chores to do," replied Little Roger, "and I started running late. That's why I missed it."

"I see," said Mr. Bellefleur, smiling. He was wearing a red flannel shirt, an old faded jean jacket, and atop his head was a John Deere cap just like the one Little Roger's dad often wore. Mr. Bellefleur was smoking as he drove.

Little Roger's mind started racing.

I'm actually in the pickup truck of the closest thing to a professional hunter. I bet Mr. Bellefleur has killed many deer, and he was probably something like nine years old when he killed his first one. Boy, I sure remember the big moose Mr. Bellefleur killed last year, too. Gosh that moose was huge. Mommy and Dad brought me and Lisa to see the big moose at Mr. Dionne's shed. I remember the eyes of the moose were still open even if the moose was dead and hanging from a large pulley.

Comfortably seated in the Dodge pickup, Little Roger found himself glancing slightly to his left to peek at the two rifles hanging from Mr. Bellefleur's gun rack inside the pickup. One of the rifles had a large scope mounted on it.

"Nice rifles, Mr. Bellefleur," said Little Roger, thinking that was a good way to lead into the many deer-hunting questions he wanted to ask the experienced hunter.

"Yes, they are, thank you," replied Mr. Bellefleur. He took a quick puff from his Marlboro cigarette. "I got this roofing job to do in Madawaska this morning. Damn job was supposed to be done last week, but I got backed up. Anyway, I think I'll be able to squeeze in some deer hunting tomorrow."

That's great, thought Little Roger. *Deer hunting.* He quickly started thinking about what deer-hunting questions he had for Mr. Bellefleur.

The Dodge pickup continued to chug along U.S. Route 1. Little Roger was thankful the pickup's heater was on because he was still cold. He wasn't so thankful, however, about the smoke from Mr. Bellefleur's cigarette.

Pépère *Long's tobacco smoke smells so good, and Dad's cigar smoke sometimes gives me a headache, but cigarette smoke is the worst,* thought Little Roger. He tried not to inhale too much of it.

"Um, tell me, Mr. Bellefleur, do you have any tips on deer hunting?" Little Roger asked in a shy manner. The cigarette smoke made him cough, but it was a short cough that wasn't too loud.

"So you're hunting deer, are you, Little Roger?" responded Mr. Bellefleur. He was smiling while still holding a cigarette between his lips. Little Roger cleared his throat. He noticed Mr. Bellefleur hadn't shaved in a day or two, and that the left breast pocket of Mr. Bellefleur's jean jacket was puffed out because it contained a small spiral notebook, a handful of pens, and a thick red carpenter's pencil.

"Well, uh, not really. I hunt rabbits and partridge," said Little Roger, "but if I see a deer, then I might take a shot at it."

Mr. Bellefleur took a quick puff on his cigarette, and then he smiled again.

"Well, Little Roger," he said, "deer are very smart animals, especially the bucks. They see and hear and smell very well. The toughest animal to hunt is deer—much harder than moose, and much harder than partridge or rabbits."

"Hmm, I see," said Little Roger.

"Little Roger, the fact is, there's deer around here, but there's also a lot of potato farms. Deer don't like some of that pesticide stuff farmers spray on their fields. That's why there's a lot more deer in Central and Southern Maine than here in the St. John Valley because we have a lot of farmers and pesticides here."

"I see," said Little Roger, absorbing it all.

Mr. Bellefleur took another puff from his cigarette.

"What type of rifle you plan on using, Little Roger? I know you're out small-game hunting, but what if you see a deer?"

"Well," said Little Roger, "I hunt with my 16-gauge shotgun."

"Is your barrel grooved?" Mr. Bellefleur immediately asked in a hurried tone.

"Grooved?" asked Little Roger.

"Yes, grooved, Little Roger. Can your 16-gauge serve as a rifle? Can you fire slugs?"

"Oh, yes, yes, Mr. Bellefleur," said Little Roger. "Yes, I can fire slugs."

"Good, good. Your 16-gauge will do, Little Roger. You can kill deer with a 16-gauge as long as you can fire slugs, but you can't be too far from the deer."

Up ahead, Little Roger saw the flashing of Frenchville's sole traffic light.

"You can drop me off at the corner, Mr. Bellefleur. I know you're heading to Madawaska. Don't worry—I can hitch a ride to St. Agatha."

"No, no, Little Roger," said Mr. Bellefleur. "I don't want you late for school. Besides, it's cold out this morning."

"But bringing me to St. Agatha is probably an extra eight miles for you, roundtrip."

"Oh, that's okay. That roofing job won't take me too long anyway."

Mr. Bellefleur flicked the pickup truck's turn signal lever up, signaling he was turning right. He eased up on the gas, applied gentle pressure on the brakes, and turned the old Dodge to the right, heading south toward St. Agatha. He puffed on his cigarette some more.

"So you want tips on deer hunting, eh, Little Roger?"

"Yes, yes sir," said Little Roger.

"Well, Little Roger, all I can tell you is what I know. Your best bet is to stand or sit still and hope you see a deer. Don't waste your time walking in the woods—deer will hear you every time. Instead, let the deer hopefully come to you."

"Yes, sir," said Little Roger.

Mr. Bellefleur started thinking fast while keeping his eye on the road. He thought of telling Little Roger about deer droppings, and how sometimes a hunter can tell where a deer has been bedding, but after quickly thinking it over he figured that discussion wasn't really necessary because Little Roger's best hope of killing a deer was to stay very quiet, hopefully see a deer, and get off a good shot. *Now, will Little Roger be close enough to get a good shot if he does see a deer?* he thought. *Fifty yards or less might do for an experienced hunter, but an eleven-year-old boy like Little Roger? With a shotgun? No more than thirty yards for Little Roger.*

"Be quiet, stay still, and wait," the experienced Mr. Bellefleur told Little Roger as the Dodge pickup headed toward the small town of St. Agatha. "Patience and the discipline to stay quiet are the two most important skills of deer hunters."

"Yes, sir," said Little Roger as he looked at Mr. Bellefleur's hands on the steering wheel.

Mr. Bellefleur has workman's hands, just like Dad's and Pépère's.

"And watch the wind currents too, Little Roger. Better to have the wind behind you, brushing against your back, because deer almost always go into the wind."

"Yes, sir," said Little Roger, absorbing all these tips.

"And don't wear anything the deer can smell. I know you're too young to shave, but don't wear any of your dad's aftershave."

"Yes, sir."

"Me—when I'm out in the woods, I don't even smoke. I have a complete set of hunting gear that's smoke-free."

"Yes, sir," replied Little Roger.

"Your best bet, Little Roger, is to sit very still and hope to get a close shot in the shoulder region of the deer. If you shoot there, that's where the deer's vital organs are."

"Okay," said Little Roger. *Shoulder region. I better remember that.*

"And be very quiet. A good shot for you will be no more than thirty yards. That's ninety feet. Anything beyond that, don't waste your time; don't shoot."

41

"Okay, I won't."

"And no aftershave," said Mr. Bellefleur. "You're not out there hunting girls, you know."

Little Roger giggled. A few seconds passed before he said, "Yes, sir."

"Killing a deer, Little Roger, is five times harder than killing a moose. They're very smart animals, deer are."

***

Ten minutes later, Mr. Bellefleur and Little Roger arrived at the parking lot of the Wisdom K to12 School in St. Agatha. Little Roger, relieved he was right on time, saw students still exiting Jim Blanchette's school bus that was parked in the parking lot.

"Thank you very much for the hunting tips, Mr. Bellefleur," said Little Roger as he stepped out of the old Dodge pickup. The cold fresh air felt good compared to the warm pickup, stuffy with cigarette smoke. "I hope the roofing job goes well and that you bag a deer this weekend."

"Thank you, Little Roger," said Mr. Bellefleur. He took a puff on his cigarette. "And good luck with your hunting, too. Just remember—be quiet and get a good shot. Who knows, maybe you'll kill a deer."

Little Roger thought: *I hope I do, Mr. Bellefleur. I hope I kill a deer and become a man.*

***

Little Roger entered the south wing of the school. He was some ten feet behind his best buddy, Ken Plourde.

"Hey, where were you when the bus stopped at your house?" Ken asked as he turned around to see Little Roger. "You missed the bus."

42

"Yeah, I know," said Little Roger. "I was running around this morning playing catch-up with things. Anyway, I hitched a ride with Mr. Bellefleur. He was kind enough to drive me all the way here even though he has a roofing job to do in Madawaska."

"That's nice of him," Ken said.

"Sure is."

Little Roger and Ken entered the school's cafeteria. They both picked up trays and utensils and got in line for breakfast.

"Pirates are coming back, eh?" said Ken as he picked up a small half-pint of milk.

"Sure are," said Little Roger. "Pops Stargell is having a good series. Plus the Pirates are loaded—Omar Moreno, the great Dave Parker, the best closer in Kent Tekulve. The Orioles are ahead right now, but things could change."

The two friends continued talking about baseball as they moved along the breakfast line. After they both got their food items, they sat at a nearby table. Soon they were joined by friends of theirs—David Michaud, Garold DuBois, the Roy brothers, Joel Gervais, Rodney Cyr, and Dale Levesque.

As they ate breakfast, Little Roger and his friends talked about the Pirates and Orioles in the World Series, and about some of their experiences during the potato harvest that had ended some two weeks prior. From time to time, Little Roger got teased by his buddies about missing the morning school bus.

***

At exactly 7:50 A.M., a loud bell rang throughout the school, the cue for all students to go to their assigned homerooms. Little Roger's homeroom class was convenient in that it also served as his first period class—Mr. Daigle's period-one reading class.

Little Roger entered his homeroom class and hung his blue jacket on one of the metal coat hooks in the back of the classroom. He then walked to his assigned desk and placed all his books inside his wooden desk except for two—his French textbook and Willa Cather's *O Pioneers!*

Little Roger started doing his French homework, which meant he started conjugating verbs—*je, tu, il, elle, nous, vous, ils, elles.*

"Stop that, Franklin!" It was Mr. Daigle's voice.

Little Roger turned around quickly and saw Franklin Bernier pulling on Mary Terriault's ponytails.

"I said, stop it, Franklin!" which Franklin Bernier did, and Little Roger resumed conjugating French verbs.

***

At 8:00 A.M. sharp, over a loudspeaker system came the voice of Don Michaud, the principal of the Wisdom K to 12 School. Mr. Michaud's morning announcement included a quick rundown of the day's scheduled activities and news items like: "Girl's varsity basketball practice will be at 3:00 P.M. followed by the boy's varsity practice which kicks off at 4:30 P.M.; the Chess Club will have a meeting today at 3:00 P.M. in Room 17; the French Club members return tomorrow from their trip to Quebec City; Fraser Paper is sponsoring a five-hundred-dollar scholarship to a graduating senior for the highest scores in chemistry." Mr. Michaud concluded his remarks by saying, "Congratulations to Tom Morin, Elaine Sirois, and Nicole LaBrie for finishing in second place in the Valley Spelling Bee. Well done, Elaine, Nicole, and Tom. And finally, today is Mrs. Celine Lavoie's birthday. Mrs. Lavoie is a twenty-one-year employee of Wisdom's cafeteria staff. Let's all wish her a happy birthday as we pass the serving line during lunch today. Happy Birthday, Celine!"

Then the school bell rang, this time signaling five minutes for students to get to their period-one class.

***

Already in the correct classroom for his period-one class, Little Roger used the five minutes to do some more French homework, and while working on those verb conjugations his mind wandered ... *Maybe this is the day I'll become a man. Patience, stay quiet, and get a close shot—that's what Mr. Bellefleur told me ... Lord, help me see one of your beautiful deer today ... I want to become a man ... I only have today after school and also tomorrow to hunt for deer because there's no hunting on Sundays, and next week we start the basketball season. It's already getting dark early now. Only today and tomorrow—two days to become a man.*

Five minutes later, the school bell rang, and Mr. Daigle began his period-one reading class.

***

"Okay, I assigned fifteen pages for today's reading," Mr. Daigle said to his students. He was standing in front of the class behind a small wooden podium.

Mr. Daigle, a tall man with a thick neck, had studied at Laval University in Quebec and also at the famous Sorbonne School in France. A lover of books and literature, the stubborn and cultured Mr. Daigle hadn't changed his curriculum when, two months earlier, some school board members complained that books like *Frankenstein, Moby Dick,* and *O Pioneers!* were "too heavy" and "deep" for eleven-year-olds.

"Can anyone tell me what the fifteen pages were about?" Mr. Daigle asked. "I know you all did the reading."

A few students raised their hands and started discussing the assigned reading.

Little Roger, sitting five rows back at his assigned desk, still kept working on his French homework, though he did have his *O Pioneers!* book open. He conjugated French verbs here and there, listened to the class discussion from time to time, and otherwise envisioned killing a deer after school.

I know exactly where I'm going to sit and wait for the deer, he reminded himself as his classmates discussed the book. *Right up Paradis Road, up about half a mile from Paul Terriault's house. There's a trail there where I've shot partridge before. There's an open meadow next to that trail. I bet deer feed there.*

"Can anyone tell me where Mr. Tovesky sent his daughter?" asked Mr. Daigle. He was still standing behind the wooden podium. "Anyone?"

Laura Gervais, who sat in the front row, raised her hand.

"Yes, Laura."

"To a convent," she said.

"That's right," Mr. Daigle said. "And why did Mr. Tovesky do that? Why did he bring his daughter to a convent?"

"Because he didn't approve of the man she was engaged to," Laura said energetically.

"Right again. Well done, Ms. Gervais." Mr. Daigle then asked, "Can anyone tell me what happened to Ms. Tovesky?"

Laura raised her hand again.

"No, no, not you, Laura. I know you know the answer. Someone else, please."

No student raised a hand.

Mr. Daigle quickly scanned the room.

"Well, there's twenty-four students here ... someone ... let's see. Roger?"

Little Roger heard his name called out and immediately his heart started racing. *Oh boy*, he thought. *I didn't hear Mr. Daigle's question.*

Dead silence.

Try to remain calm, he reminded himself. *Plus, last night's reading wasn't all that bad; I enjoyed part of it.*

"Yes?" said Little Roger, hoping such an open inquiry would prompt a repeat of the question from Mr. Daigle.

"Roger, what happened to the girl who went to the convent?"

Whew thought Little Roger. *Okay, at least now I know the question ... but ... but what's the answer? Last night's reading was my favorite from* O Pioneers! *because part of the reading involved a baseball game.*

Little Roger cleared his throat. "Well I know Amedee was a good baseball pitcher," he said, smiling.

Some classmates laughed. Mr. Daigle tried to hold back a smile.

"Yes, Roger, I know you liked reading about the baseball game," said Mr. Daigle. "But what about the girl? Her name was Marie. Her dad took her to a convent. What eventually happened to her?"

Little Roger started focusing on last night's reading. He actually knew about the father bringing his daughter to the convent, but when he thought about this all he could remember was that the convent was in St. Louis.

"Anyone want to help out Roger?"

Laura Gervais was eager to help, but she didn't raise her hand because she figured she'd be shot down again by Mr. Daigle.

Focus ... focus ...

"Oh yeah, I know—I know," said Little Roger in excitement. "I remember what happened to her."

"Go ahead, Roger," said Mr. Daigle.

"She married the guy anyway. Marie ran off with him, and her father forgave her."

"Right you are, Roger," said Mr. Daigle in an approving tone. "Good to know you read the whole assignment and not just the part about the baseball game."

Whew, thought Little Roger. *Thank God I remembered that stuff from last night's reading. What triggered my memory was the fact that the guy Marie eventually married was at first a lazy sort of man, but then, when Marie's father forgave her, Marie's father actually bought the new young couple a farm, and that's when Marie's husband started working very hard—"like a devil" was how Willa Cather described how hard he worked. Boy oh boy, what saved me was when I read that portion of the story, I envisioned some St. John Valley farmers working hard like demons. Then when Mr. Daigle asked me the question the image of a farmer turning into a demon finally popped in my head. That's how I remember how that lazy guy started working hard, and that led to Marie's father forgiving Marie because her new husband turned out all right.*

Happy and relieved, Little Roger went back to conjugating French verbs and daydreaming about deer hunting.

***

"Okay, good work, gang," said Mr. Daigle when the school bell rang signaling the end of period one. "Please read the next fifteen pages of *O Pioneers!* Everyone have a good and safe weekend."

Little Roger, like the rest of his classmates, got up, opened his wooden desk drawer, and exchanged his period-one materials for his upcoming period-two class—Mr. Bechard's science class.

Seconds later, the school bell rang, the cue for students to be at their next class in five minutes.

***

Lester Bechard, a slim and fit man of thirty-eight, found his true calling as a teacher. After a six-year stint in the Navy, he returned to his native Valley and began taking college courses at the University of Maine at Fort Kent. It was there he eventually earned his teacher's certification.

Intense and passionate, Bechard decided to teach sixth-grade science primarily because he believed "young students need exposure to science at an early age." And as a big believer in group thinking and group projects, Bechard often assembled his students in teams of four to work collectively on science problems. That's how Little Roger found himself teamed up with Gerry Daigle, Bruce Lavoie, and Dennis Pelletier that Friday morning. The foursome busily worked throughout the class period on their four assigned homework problems, problems that all involved plants and photosynthesis.

"I expect four answers from each group," Bechard instructed the class. "Carefully go over the four problems I assigned yesterday and come up with one group answer for each problem."

***

With fifteen minutes left in the class, Mr. Bechard discussed, in great detail, what the correct answers were to the problems and how they should be derived. Little Roger listened attentively to Mr. Bechard's explanations. He also took good notes and discovered where he and his group had gone wrong with one of the science problems.

Then the sound of the school bell again.

Boy, period two already over with, thought Little Roger as he heard the school bell ring. *And I didn't have any time to think about deer hunting because Mr. Bechard always keeps us busy.*

Mr. Bechard assigned another four science problems immediately after the school bell rang, and after he gave the assignment Little Roger got up, exited the room, and went to his homeroom (Mr. Daigle's room) to exchange his science textbook for his history one. When the school bell rang again, Little Roger was in his assigned seat in David Morneau's period-three history class.

***

"Good morning everyone," said Mr. Morneau as he entered the classroom.

"Good morning, Mr. Morneau," replied the students.

Last night's reading was about JFK and LBJ. It was interesting, Little Roger reminded himself as he opened his history textbook to page 89. *I hope Mr. Morneau calls on me today.*

"Remember, class, your papers must be at least ten pages in length," Mr. Morneau said as he took a seat behind his sizeable gray-metal desk, which occupied the front east corner of the classroom. "Papers will be due in about a month. Okay, let's get started on the reading assignment I gave you."

Mr. Morneau started discussing the assigned reading, and Little Roger was absorbing it all because he was interested in the subject matter. The JFK assassination, LBJ in the White House, the push for civil rights—all were interesting topics for Little Roger.

"Make sure you guys write this down," Mr. Morneau advised his students as he wrote down important facts, themes, and dates on the large blackboard behind him. "You may see some of these remarks on the next exam. Many of you did well on our last exam, but some of you didn't. Remember, every question on exams is something we covered in class. And dates and people and when things occurred are important. History is about remembering important events and movements."

On it went like this for the next forty minutes—Mr. Morneau going over the reading and writing down important facts, dates, and themes on the blackboard. Occasionally, he'd ask his students questions, too.

Shoot. Mr. Morneau hasn't called on me yet, thought a frustrated Little Roger. *And I knew the answers to almost all of the questions he's asked. He even asked, "Where was LBJ sworn in as President?" I figured he'd ask that one, and I raised my hand, but he didn't call on me.*

"What are some of the similarities between Presidents Johnson and Carter?" Mr. Morneau asked. There were about ten minutes left in the class period.

Little Roger raised his hand, but Mr. Morneau called on Brian LaBrie.

"Yes, Brian, go ahead."

"They were both farmers," said Brian, the son of Reno LaBrie, a St. Agatha potato farmer.

"Well, that's not exactly right," said Mr. Morneau, "but you're partly right. President Carter was a farmer. I don't think President Johnson was ever a farmer." Mr. Morneau then asked, "Can anyone name the type of farming President Carter did before he became president?"

Five hands shot up.

"Okay, okay, go ahead Dale," said Mr. Morneau, pointing to Dale Collin.

"He was a peanut farmer."

"That's right," said Mr. Morneau.

51

Then Jay Morin raised his hand.

"Yes, Jay."

"But President Johnson owned a big ranch in Texas. Ranching is farming."

Mr. Morneau digested that comment for a couple of seconds.

"Well ... well, that's true," he said. "Yes, I guess President Johnson may qualify as a farmer. Good point, Jay. Brian—I guess you were right. President Johnson qualifies as a farmer."

A brief moment of silence ensued, and then Mr. Morneau asked, "Anyone else? What are the similarities between President Johnson and President Carter?"

No hands went up. Little Roger started thinking fast. *Gosh darnit—I knew a lot of the answers all morning, but right now nothing comes to mind with this similarities stuff.*

More seconds passed, and still no one raised a hand.

Wait—I know! Little Roger raised his hand.

"Yes, Roger, go ahead," said Mr. Morneau.

"They are both Democrats," said Little Roger, smiling and confident.

"Yes, that's true," Mr. Morneau said. "President Johnson was a Democrat, and so is our current president. Good answer. Anyone else?"

More silence and no raised hands. Little Roger had another thought. He was confident about this one, too, so he raised his hand again.

"Yes, Roger. You have another similarity for us?"

"Yes, Mr. Morneau, I do. Both Presidents Carter and Johnson are from the South. They are Southerners, unlike Kennedy, who was from New England."

"Yes, that's true, Roger. Both Presidents Carter and Johnson come from the South. Good job. And now that you've mentioned

President Kennedy, can anyone name President Kennedy's home state?"

Little Roger raised his hand. Once again, his was the only raised hand.

"No, not you, Roger—I'm sure you know the answer. Anyone? C'mon now class, this is about President Kennedy, the only Catholic president we've ever had, and Roger gave away a clue in his last answer by saying President Kennedy was from New England, which is true. Anyone?"

Gail Cyr raised her hand.

"Yes, Gail," said Mr. Morneau.

"Was President Kennedy from Connecticut?"

"No, Gail, I'm sorry, that's not correct," said Mr. Morneau. "President Kennedy was not from Connecticut. I know many of you here have relatives in Connecticut, relatives of yours who went south to Connecticut in search of good-paying manufacturing jobs. But no, Connecticut is not the right answer. Anyone else?"

Brenda Albert tried her luck and raised her hand.

"Yes, Brenda," said Mr. Morneau.

"New Hampshire. President Kennedy was from New Hampshire."

"No, I'm sorry, that's not right either," said Mr. Morneau. "New Hampshire is a beautiful state, but it's not President Kennedy's home state."

Then Monique Michaud raised her hand.

"Okay, Monique," Mr. Morneau said. "Do you know President Kennedy's home state?"

"Well, it's in New England, right, and it's not Connecticut or New Hampshire," said Monique. "I also don't think it's Maine, because we would know if it were Maine. I don't think it's Rhode Island, because Rhode Island is very small. Is it Massachusetts?"

"Yes, Monique, you're right," said Mr. Morneau. "Good process of elimination, too. Yes, President Kennedy was from Massachusetts. And let me remind this class that Monique did a great job eliminating possible answers. Remember that technique on the multiple choice portions of your history exams."

Shortly thereafter, the school bell rang signaling the end of period three. When the bell stopped ringing, Mr. Morneau gave the reading assignment for the weekend.

"Have a good weekend, and remember to read pages 105 to 120. And pay particular attention to the Vietnam War. The Vietnam War will be our focus next week."

Little Roger opened his history notebook and wrote, *Read pages 105-120.* Then he thought, *Shoot, I left my assignment notebook in my desk. What was our reading assignment? Hmm? ... Oh yeah, read next fifteen pages of* O Pioneers! *For science? Hmm? ... Oh yeah, do next four problems.*

Little Roger wrote those entries in his history notebook, and then he got up like the other students and started exiting the classroom to go to his period-four class.

"Did you read the *National Geographic* article about the Valley, Little Roger?" asked Mr. Morneau. He was standing next to the classroom door as Little Roger was just about to walk past him. "You know, a team from *National Geographic* came to the Valley three years ago."

"Yes, Mr. Morneau. I read it last year," said Little Roger. "We have the issue at home because my parents always subscribe to the *National Geographic*. I will read the article again, though, to help me with my paper."

"Good, that's a good idea, Roger."

Suddenly, a thought hit Little Roger. *Mr. Morneau will like this.*

"I'll be sure to include the story about your Uncle Claude in my paper, Mr. Morneau, and how he saved himself and his buddies in North Africa during World War II."

"Oh that's great, Roger," Mr. Morneau said, joy written all over his face. "Did you read the *St. John Valley Times* article on that? They did interview my uncle, you know."

"Yes, yes I did," Little Roger said proudly. He then had another thought.

"And in my paper, I'll be sure to mention how your grandparents had twenty kids, with seven of your uncles serving in World War II all at the same time."

"Oh, that's nice, Roger. Yes, my grandparents did have twenty children. Of course, my father was too young to serve during the Second World War, but he would have if he had been old enough."

***

Little Roger's next class was English taught by Mr. Ed Bosse, a short slim man who also coached the girls' junior varsity basketball team.

Once he entered Mr. Bosse's classroom, Little Roger placed a five-subject notebook on a desk. He took a seat at the desk and opened up the notebook.

I started my history-paper outline last night in this notebook, he thought. *I'll use this class period to add to that outline.*

Forty minutes into the class period, Mr. Bosse selected Susan Chamberland, a petite blond, to "tell the entire class, Susan, what you've been working on this period."

Susan—widely considered the best writer and most articulate speaker in the class—had written a poem, a poem about a smart student who gets teased by her classmates for getting good grades. Little Roger listened to Susan's poem here and there, but he mostly continued working on his history paper outline. He was relieved Mr. Bosse hadn't called on him to read his most recent work.

"Very good, Susan, that was great," said Mr. Bosse after Susan had finished reading her short poem. Mr. Bosse was standing in the back of the class with his arms folded over his chest. "Excellent work. That was a nice poem, Susan," he said. "Let's all give Susan a round of applause."

Little Roger and his classmates clapped as Susan, who had read her poem standing up, sat back down at her desk.

"Okay, something a little different today," said Mr. Bosse. "Let's hear from someone else."

Gosh darn—my luck, Little Roger immediately thought. *That's new, calling upon two students to read out loud. We never had that before.* He crossed his fingers, hoping he wouldn't be called upon.

"Roger, we know you're working on a history paper," said Mr. Bosse. "What did you write today during class?"

Oh no ... gosh darnit, thought Little Roger. *Why did Mr. Bosse have to pick on me?* He felt his face blush; he could hear and feel his heart pounding. *Boy ... gosh ... I ... I wrote very little. I mostly fine-tuned my outline and added to it some.*

Nervous, he slowly stood up. In a shaky voice, he said, "Well, I'm, uh, I'm working on the history paper Mr. Morneau assigned us yesterday. Uh ... my history paper has to be longer, and it has to be about the St. John Valley."

He knew his voice sounded nervous and bad, but he continued.

"Uh, Mr. Bosse, I really don't have anything to read because I'm still working on the outline for the paper." Little Roger then mustered the courage to say, "Uh, Mr. Bosse, I'd hate to read from sections of my paper that aren't complete."

There was silence.

"Very well then, Roger," said Mr. Bosse. He was still standing in the back of the classroom, his arms crossed over his chest. "What exactly is your history paper about?"

"Well, uh, like I said, it's about the St. John Valley. I've got stories in my paper that my parents told me about. I also have my family histories in my paper."

"I see," said Mr. Bosse. "Well, Roger, is there any theme in your paper? Or maybe you can tell us a story or two that's in your paper?"

Little Roger started thinking fast. *A theme? Hmm?* Nothing came to mind. This forced him to just say the first thing that popped in his head.

"Well, uh, for example one short story—a very short story— is one I use to help me describe St. Agatha's Long Lake. We all know what happens during the winter months to Long Lake: it freezes, of course. It's not uncommon for snowmobiles, cars, even big lumber trucks to drive on the frozen ice of Long Lake during the winter. It's also common to see many of the small wooden cabins—the ice-fishing cabins—on the lake, especially near the Sporting Club restaurant in St. Agatha, because there's good ice fishing there."

Little Roger noticed most of his classmates listening to him attentively.

"Well, we all know about frozen lakes, ice fishing, and ice-fishing cabins because we're from here, and we see these cabins every winter. But my dad once told me a story he heard from a St. Agatha potato farmer. In fact, it was your father, Greg."

Little Roger quickly looked at Greg Martin, a bespectacled straight-A student and often the class's top academic performer. Greg looked at Little Roger attentively and with a smile.

"Greg, your father told my dad this story. See, Mr. Martin and his work crew were busy loading potatoes in a big tractor-trailer truck. Of course, this was in the winter—last winter in fact—because we all know that potatoes are shipped out in the winter months. Well anyway, the tractor-trailer driver was a big black man from Alabama. This big truck driver at one point got out of his truck to catch the winter scenery. After walking around a bit, the truck driver walked up to Mr. Martin and told him, 'My, y'all have some nice flat land here in Northern Maine.' Of course, he was looking at Long Lake, which was frozen and perfectly flat for miles. 'Yep, nice flat land here in Northern Maine,' said this truck driver to Mr. Martin while he was still looking at the frozen lake. 'I bet you those are nice potato fields in the summer.' And that's when Mr. Martin led the truck driver on and said, 'Oh yes, those are our nice potato fields just covered with snow right now.' And then the truck driver asked, 'But tell me, sir, who lives in those tiny wooden cabins on that nice flat land? That ain't much for houses now, is it?' Of course, the truck driver was referring to the small ice-fishing cabins on frozen Long Lake. And Mr. Martin told him, 'Oh, those small houses. Those small houses are for poor people on welfare. They work in the potato fields for us.'"

Some classmates, including Greg, laughed. Little Roger smiled. He quickly looked over at Mr. Bosse, who was smiling too.

"So I use stories like that to describe Long Lake and the St. John Valley," Little Roger said confidently, "because not everybody has ever seen a frozen lake."

"Very good," said Mr. Bosse, "very good. Anymore stories, Roger?"

Little Roger thought the class period should have been over by now, but he looked at the clock on the wall directly ahead of him.

Five minutes to go, he thought. He started thinking fast. He looked at his outline. One word that got his attention was *changes*.

Changes. If there's a theme to my paper, that might be it.

"Uh, well, the more I think about it, if there is a theme to my paper, then it's about the changes that have taken place in the St. John Valley."

"What type of changes?" asked Mr. Bosse.

"Well, there's really a lot of them," said Little Roger. He glanced at his paper outline under the word *changes*.

Farming.

"Take, for example, farming," he said. "Forty years ago, just about everyone was a farmer—at least there were a lot more farmers back then. For example, my dad told me Mr. Bea Daigle has bought out twenty-three farmers so far, and he's not even the largest farmer in Frenchville. Farming is getting more and more mechanized, too, with less farmworkers needed to do the work."

Little Roger caught a glimpse of classmates Paul Charette, Brian LaBrie, Allen Terriault, and Greg Martin—all classmates whose fathers were potato farmers. He saw Brian LaBrie nod in approval.

"Three weeks ago, many of us in this classroom were in potato fields picking potatoes. That's why all the schools in the St. John Valley—both the American and the Canadian schools—shut down from early September to early October, because of the potato-picking harvest, and because farmers need students like us to pick potatoes. But more and more farmers now have harvesters made by International Harvester or John Deere companies like that. A harvester with five workers can replace something like eighty potato pickers. My dad recently told me that probably in five or ten years from now there won't be a need for schools to close down for the potato harvest because all the farmers will have harvesters. So technology is changing farming a lot. That's a big change."

"That's interesting, Roger," said Mr. Bosse. "We've got about another two minutes or so left in class. Anything else? Any other changes you'll write about in your paper?"

Little Roger quickly glanced at his history paper outline again.

Catholic Church.

"Yes sir," said Little Roger in a confident tone. "An area with a lot of changes is the Catholic Church. My parents—especially my dad—remember when Mass was only in Latin. There was no French and no English Mass—everything in Latin. In fact, at St. Luce Parish in Frenchville, English Mass just started this past summer. I started being an altar boy when I was eight years old, and I never heard Mass in English, only French. That's why Father Levesque had to teach all the altar boys the prayers and the prayer responses in English this past summer, because none of us know how to pray in English. Also, not only was Mass only in French until this summer, but Mass was always on Sunday, too. I never experienced Saturday Mass until Father Levesque changed that, too, this past summer. So now, at St. Luce Parish, we have English Mass on Saturdays and French Mass on Sundays. That's a big change. I think all the Valley parishes, especially the American ones, added English and Saturday Mass, too. My parents told me that when they were growing up, Mass was completely in Latin, and the parishioners knew what to recite and say, but they really didn't know or understand what they were saying because no one knew Latin, except the priests, of course. So the Catholic Church is changing a lot, and the Valley is very Catholic."

"That's interesting, Roger," Mr. Bosse said in an approving tone. "Sounds like you've got a lot to write about. Anything else, Roger?"

"Well, there are some other subjects, but the theme of changes is a big one, sir. For example, my parents remember when almost no one went to college, but now we see more and more high-school graduates going to college."

"Yes, that's true," Mr. Bosse said.

"Oh, and my dad remembers when there was a lot less regulation in the farming business. Right now, environmental laws are getting stricter and stricter. For example, a farmer needs a permit to spray pesticides on potato fields, and whoever is doing the spraying has to attend a class to get certified, too. That's a new regulation that just took place last year."

"That's interesting," said Mr. Bosse, and just as he said that the school bell rang signaling the end of period four and the start of the lunch period.

***

Little Roger spent his fifty-minute lunch period with his good buddies Ken Plourde, Garold DuBois, Dale Dugal, Joel Michaud, Rodney Morin, David Boucher, Glen Gervais, and the Roy brothers. The lunches consisted of codfish with tartar sauce, hot roll, buttered corn, and milk, and after lunch the friends all played basketball on the school's front asphalt parking lot.

The particular basketball game they played was "Make It, Take It": first team to ten points wins; winning team must win by two points; each basket counts one point. Two teams quickly formed up.

Paula Pelletier and Sheila Martin were on opposing teams, and though Paula and Sheila were girls, they were better basketball players than most of the boys. Paula was especially sought after because she had a nice jump shot.

Ten minutes into the game, the score was tied at eight, but then the school bell rang signaling the end of the lunch recess

61

period. That's when Jacques Roy said, "Okay, we all know the winning team is supposed to win by two points, but we ain't got enough time for that. Next basket wins."

Everyone agreed.

Joel Michaud, twelve years old and already six feet tall, drove hard to the basket but missed a tough short hook, probably because he had three defenders on him. Ken Plourde picked up the rebound, dished out a quick pass to Dave Boucher who in turn found Paula Pelletier open for a jumper.

Swish—perfect.

"Game over," declared Jacques Roy. "Nice shot, Paula."

Little Roger, who was in charge of defending Dave Boucher, was on the losing team.

***

Little Roger still had a few sentences to conjugate when he entered Mr. Lavoie's fifth-period French class. That didn't worry him, though, not with Mr. Lavoie's system of always asking questions in a set order (basically, he called upon students up and down the row of seats ... "next student" ... "next student" ... that way, the students always knew when it was their turn to answer; they always knew when they'd be called upon). And when Little Roger wasn't called upon, he finished conjugating those last sentences, and, once he finished those, he thought about the details of his upcoming hunt ... how he'd wait patiently—*patience is key to deer hunting*; how he'd give himself a good field of fire—*I don't want trees or branches in the way of my shot*; how he'd think of important details—*put a slug in the shotgun, not birdshot, and remember wind currents ...*

After fifty minutes of listening to verb conjugations and daydreaming about killing a deer to become a man, Little Roger heard the class bell ring. He placed his French grammar book and class notebook in his book bag and headed toward his period-six class. Five minutes later, Little Roger was seated in Mr. Boucher's math class.

***

There were four reasons why math—Little Roger's toughest class—went by relatively fast that particular Friday afternoon. First, just as in some of his previous classes, Little Roger found himself thinking about his deer-hunting plans from time to time, and thinking about something he was actually excited about seemed to make time pass by quickly. Secondly, Mr. Boucher spent most of the class period working math problems on the blackboard, and here Little Roger often found himself paying close attention to Mr. Boucher's problem analysis because Little Roger wanted to make sure he understood what was going on. Third, Little Roger occasionally couldn't help but look at Emily Levesque, who sat just one seat to his left. Little Roger secretly had a crush on Emily, and he couldn't help but admire how she was developing from a girl to a woman. Only his good buddy Ken Plourde knew of his crush on Emily. Little Roger had confided that fact to Ken the previous week when the two friends made a pact: "Tell me the girl you like and I'll tell you the girl I like, and let's keep this between us ... promise you won't tell anyone else." Little Roger's crush was Emily; Ken's crush was Brenda Sirois.

Finally, Little Roger's period-six class went by relatively fast because he was anxious for his next and last class of the day—physical education, his favorite class of all.

After fifty minutes of math equations, some daydreaming about deer hunting, occasional observations of the beautiful Emily, and an anxiousness to play sports, the class bell rang and

Little Roger, like the other students in his class, quickly walked to the other end of the school building where the gymnasium was located.

***

After changing into the mandatory gym attire of shorts, white T-shirt, and sneakers, Little Roger joined his classmates for stretching exercises on the indoor basketball court. After five minutes of stretches and exercises, Joe Dugal, the physical education instructor and coach of the girls' varsity basketball team, had the students form up into two teams.

"Okay gang," said the five-foot-five, barrel-chested Dugal in a loud authoritative voice. "Today we're playing basketball."

A Korean War veteran who sported a full head of jet-black hair, Dugal was in many ways Wisdom's K to 12 School's version of Bobby Knight, the famed tough and demanding coach of the Indiana University men's basketball team. With a reputation for yelling at referees and barking orders to his players, Dugal definitely got his fair share of technical fouls. But also like Bobby Knight, the emotional and passionate Dugal was absolutely and completely committed to his players, and his coaching style, like Knight's, produced solid results: in three of the last four years, Dugal's girls' varsity basketball team made the playoffs, and they reached the Eastern Maine finals twice.

"Okay—team one players, you guys wear these numbered yellow vests," Dugal said as he passed out the vests to nine players. "For anybody that's not wearing a vest, that means you're on team two. When I blow the whistle, then all players on the court are replaced by another squad of players from their respective teams. We'll also have one-for-one substitutions if necessary. The goal is for everyone to play."

Dugal paused for a second or two. He started checking out the two teams, ensuring they were balanced talent-wise, and then he said a phrase he was renowned for: "Losing team will owe the winning team fifty push-ups because losing ain't an option."

***

After thirty minutes of basketball, Coach Dugal blew his whistle and announced, "Game over, game over," and though Little Roger had a good game—he scored three baskets, pulled down a couple rebounds, and had some good passes—he still found himself on the losing team.

"Losing team owes the winning team fifty push-ups, because losing ain't an option," Dugal said. "Losers—fifty push-ups, now! That will teach you guys to try harder next time and to play better defense." And then Dugal said something his players and students had heard many times before, another one of his oft-quoted lines: "You all remind me when I was in Korea. All I remember was, we were fighting the North Koreans and we were heading south. That ain't no way to defend a peninsula; that ain't no defense."

***

After showering and putting on his school clothes again, Little Roger returned to his homeroom class with the rest of his classmates. Once there, he placed his homework books in his book bag and waited for the final bell to ring—the final bell being the signal that he could get on his assigned school bus and go home.

I know the perfect place to wait for a deer—up the ridge about half a mile from Mr. Terriault's house, he thought as he sat at his desk and waited to hear that final bell. *Patience is very important. That's what Mr. Bellefleur advised me ...*

Consider the wind currents ...

Don't shoot if the deer is more than thirty yards away ...

Shoot the deer in the shoulder region ...

The final bell rang, and as soon as it did, Little Roger and his friends ran out of the school building and hopped on one of three school buses—either the St. Agatha/Sinclair bus, the Frenchville bus heading toward Madawaska, or the Frenchville bus heading toward Fort Kent. Little Roger appropriately got on the Frenchville bus heading west toward Fort Kent.

I don't care to see rabbits or partridge, Little Roger thought shortly after getting on the school bus. *If I see rabbits or partridge, I won't shoot them, because that will scare away any deer. And I'm just hunting with my slug shots, too.*

"Hey, Little Roger. We're playing touch football Saturday afternoon on the old Dr. Levesque School playing field." Little Roger recognized the voice right away—it was that of David Boucher, a fourteen-year-old who lived some ten houses from Little Roger's home. The school-bus ride had just gotten under way.

"Game's at two P.M., okay?"

Little Roger looked behind himself and saw David. He thought quickly: *Darnit—this is my only weekend to deer hunt, to become a man, because basketball season kicks off next week and it gets dark early now. I've got this afternoon and Saturday to become a man. Maybe I shouldn't play football Saturday afternoon. But me and my friends always play sports on weekends. Plus, if I say no, they'll know something's up, and they'll ask me why I can't play. I don't want to lie, Lord.*

"Uh, hmm—sure, Dave. Who's coming?" Little Roger asked.

"Oh we've got a great lineup. Ken here, Garold, Rodney, myself, Joe Tardiff, the Roys, Paula, Sheila, my sister Ann, my brothers Gary and Phil, Dale Dugal, and Glen Gervais, too—the whole crew," Boucher said.

Ken Plourde, who shared the bus seat with Dave Boucher, chimed in with, "Yeah, Roger, you gotta come play football tomorrow afternoon."

"Great—count me in," said Little Roger, trying to sound excited.

"See ya at two P.M. behind the Dr. Levesque School," said Dave.

"Yeah, I'll see you guys there," said Little Roger.

Little Roger slouched down in his school bus seat. *Boy, I sure better get that deer this afternoon or tomorrow morning. If I don't show up for the football game, my friends will ask me where I was—why I missed the game.*

The bus kept headed northwest on Route 162 toward Frenchville. Many students busied themselves by talking to their friends, and everyone seemed to be in a good mood—it was Friday, after all. Little Roger, Ken, and Dave started talking about the World Series and next year's Boston Red Sox. Then suddenly ...

"Yes, I know what I saw. I read it in the *St. John Valley Times*," said Jacques Roy. "It was for drunk driving last week."

Doug Michaud, who was sitting in one of the middle seats, yelled, "Shut up, Jacques. Just shut the hell up."

"Make me," said Jacques in a taunting tone. "Dee-You-Eye—that's driving under the influence. And your father's name was right there. It was in the *St. John Valley Times*. Hey everybody, Doug Michaud's dad got busted for drunk driving last week."

Some students immediately smiled, the type of smile that means someone has knowledge about an embarrassing fact. A few students also laughed. Doug Michaud's face turned red. He stood up as if he was going to fight Jacques Roy, but Jacques was a bit older and much, much bigger. Doug sat down in his bus seat.

Little Roger didn't smile. Nor did he laugh. He thought, *Everybody reads the* St. John Valley Times. *That small newspaper helps gossip circulate throughout the Valley. Who got arrested for what, who got a DUI, who went bankrupt ... everybody knows everybody else's business.*

The schoolchildren on the bus went back to their chit-chatting, and Little Roger, Ken, and Dave resumed their talk about baseball and the Pirates versus Orioles World Series.

***

The school bus stopped in front of Little Roger's home at exactly 3:20 P.M. Little Roger got off the bus and started walking up the asphalt driveway of his parents' home, and after a few steps he stopped, turned around, and waved goodbye to his friends who were still on the bus. He turned around again to resume walking up the driveway, and that's when he saw his father, Bob, in the cement-floored garage organizing garden tools. It was easy for Little Roger to see his father because the garage door was wide open.

"Hi, Dad," Little Roger said to his father as he walked up the driveway. "You're home early."

"Well, hello there, young feller," said Bob as he removed a short-stub King Edward cigar from his mouth. "Yes, I'm home early. I just worked half a shift today. I was filling in for a friend—he just needed me to work half his shift."

"Dad, I'm gonna go for a quick hunt," said Little Roger as he entered the garage. His voice was excited. "I'll be back for supper, so don't worry."

"Well, as long as you're back for dinner, it's okay," said Bob. He placed an empty gas container on the cement floor. "Just remember—it gets dark out early."

"Yes, Dad," said Little Roger.

Little Roger entered the house and went straight to his bedroom. He placed his book bag on his desk, and then he started to undress. *This may very well be the day. God, help me see a deer. If I kill a deer this afternoon, I'll be a man. Oh boy!*

Those were some of his thoughts as he was changing into his hunting clothes. He moved quickly and with a sense of purpose.

Okay, I'm all set to go, Little Roger told himself in his bedroom. He was doing his last-minute checks.

Got my proper hunting clothes—old faded jeans, work boots, red sweatshirt, bright orange hooded hunter's coat, and my orange hunter's cap.

He knelt down, reached underneath his bed, and grabbed his shotgun and shells. He placed the slugs in his coat, and then he stood up and did his final check: *three slugs in my left coat pocket and three slugs in my right pocket.* He reminded himself: *I'm not hunting partridge or rabbits this afternoon.* He then knelt down again, made a sign of the cross, and prayed the following: *Dear Lord, I want to be a man, and I've already prayed to you about what I have to do to accomplish this. I love all your creatures, Lord—both big and small—and I respect your beautiful deer a lot, too. They are great animals with great senses. I hope this is not a sin, Lord—killing a deer. I know killing a deer is not sin when you need the food, but I know my family doesn't need me to kill a deer for food. Well, I hope I'm not committing sin, Lord. If I am, I apologize for that, and I'm confessing it now. I need to do this to be a man, Lord.*

Thank you for everything, and help us find Bill in Panama. Amen.

Little Roger exited his bedroom and went to the garage. He started walking down the driveway, and in just a few seconds he had crossed U.S. Route 1 and headed in a southeasterly direction.

I know exactly where I'll situate myself to hunt, he reminded himself as he walked through an open field. *Right next to that batch of pine trees up a ridge about half a mile from Paradis Road. It's right at the beginning of a trail, and there's a small stream maybe fifty yards away. That'll be my spot, and hopefully that's where I'll kill a deer and become a man.*

***

Little Roger came upon a narrow brook that had to be crossed. *No problem,* he thought. *That brook can't be more than four feet wide. I'll just run a little to give myself momentum to jump over it.*

He started to take a few quick steps, then he accelerated ... and ...

Darnit ... my left boot is now soaked, he realized as soon as he cleared the brook. Loose slippery mud at the edge of the brook had compromised his footing, which made him clear less distance from his jump. *Right boot's muddy—that's okay, but my left boot landed in the brook. Gosh, that water's cold. My left boot and foot are soaked and cold from that brook water.* He kept walking in a southeasterly direction, and he immediately noticed his steps with his left foot producing a squishing sound.

I guess I'm squeezing the water out of my boot. He kept walking.

Minutes later, Little Roger found himself walking through the soft earth of one of Bea Daigle's recently harvested potato fields. Up ahead, he could see the Desjardin buckwheat farm.

That's where the staff of the National Geographic *magazine stayed,* he thought as he continued walking briskly. *They stayed at the Desjardin Farm. The writers and photographers—they stayed with the Desjardins. That was two years ago.* National Geographic *did a nice segment on the St. John Valley. I sure better re-read that article because all I remember was the article focusing on old-fashioned stuff like people picking potatoes in a field or seeing a horse-and-buggy. Some of our neighbors thought the article made residents of the Valley seem old-fashioned, backward, and poor. That article didn't mention many farmers switching to modern tractors and replacing potato pickers with machine harvesters.*

He kept walking. His still-wet left foot and boot were both cold, but at least he wasn't making the squishing sound anymore. *Like Mr. Bellefleur told me this morning—I gotta be quiet if I want to see and shoot a deer.*

In no time, Little Roger found himself walking slightly uphill and following a tree line that served as a border between a meadow and thick woods. As he kept walking, he soon saw the very spot where he had shot and killed a partridge the previous year.

I'm not interested in small game—not today or tomorrow, he reminded himself. He continued walking briskly, and minutes later he saw the opening of a wide trail heading into the woods. He took the trail and kept walking.

Won't be long now, he told himself. *I'll be fortunate to get a full hour's worth of hunting this afternoon, because I know the sun sets fast.*

He saw a batch of pine trees up ahead. He took a few more steps, and then he saw a meadow and the beginning of another trail in the woods.

My spot is next to those pine trees, he reminded himself. He kept walking, and soon he saw a huge clearing to his left, a clearing needed because of the power lines cutting through the woods.

I don't think power lines affect deer, do they? He kept walking. *Maybe I should have discussed my hunting spot in detail with Mr. Bellefleur. Anyway, that power line is pretty far out, maybe an eighth of a mile from my spot.*

He kept walking up the trail, and then suddenly, a thought hit him:

Did I load my shotgun? No, no I didn't. Stupid me. Darn good thing I haven't seen anything yet because if I did, I probably wouldn't have had time to load my shotgun.

Little Roger kept walking, and as he did he reached down into the right-hand pocket of his orange jacket and picked up a slug. He cracked open his gun's barrel and properly loaded the slug, all while still walking and observing his surroundings.

After a minute or so, Little Roger stopped walking. He took a long look to his left to see the power-line clearing again, and as he turned his head to the right to see up ahead, he saw a small reddish animal lying down near the opening of the trail next to the pine trees. He continued walking forward, but much slower now, and he kept his eyes fixated on the small animal.

What a beautiful fox that is, he thought as he kept walking forward. He quickly figured the reddish-brown fox with the white-tip tail was some sixty yards away.

No way will I shoot a fox, he thought. *Besides, foxes are for trapping, not shooting.* Pépère *Long traps them—the beautiful fox, the beautiful* renard.

He kept walking forward slowly. The fox was lying down comfortably right next to the start of the wood line and another trail. Little Roger noticed that the opening of that trail was dark because it led to deep thick woods, mostly fir trees. Little Roger kept walking forward and observing the fox.

Gosh, what a beautiful animal that is, he thought as he kept walking toward the fox. *It's not very big, too. Its tail is huge, but its body is small. No way does that beautiful fox weigh fifty pounds. I'm guessing it's more like thirty pounds.*

He kept walking forward, knowing that at some point the fox would scoot away. He also knew the sun—and with it the temperature—were both going down.

Sunset will be in an hour, max, he thought as he kept walking and observing the fox. *And I know exactly where the sun will set, too—right between those two hills, out to the west toward Fort Kent.*

Suddenly, the fox scooted away, and Little Roger thought, *Goodbye, fox.* He figured he was about fifty yards from the fox. He was amazed at how quickly and silently the fox got up and left.

Little Roger kept walking forward. *Will deer be turned off by the sight and smell of a fox? Who was it—Uncle Gilles or Mr. Voisine?—who told me two years ago that deer are attracted to the smell of urine? Did that include fox urine, or was it just doe urine that the bucks like? Gosh darn, maybe deer will be turned off by that beautiful fox I just saw.*

He kept walking forward as he pondered the once close proximity of the fox and its potential for scaring away deer.

Well, I don't have time to plan another hunting spot, especially not with the sun setting. Hmm? I hope foxes don't scare away deer.

When he arrived at his planned hunting spot—a spot some one hundred feet from where the fox had been resting—Little

Roger quickly glanced at his surroundings. The fox was nowhere in sight. Sporadically, he heard breezes wisp by, but that was it for sounds. Suddenly, he smelled the nearby pine trees, and the smell reminded him of hunting with his brother, Bill, two years earlier.

Panama sure is far away from here, he thought as he scanned the woods for a proper place to either sit or stand. *I hope we hear from Bill soon.*

More scanning of the woods, then a thought: *This is good, this is good—the fall foliage here in northern Maine is well over with. The woods are gray, the trees have no leaves ... at least the hardwoods have no leaves. That's good because I can see well into the woods and meadow. It's easier to hunt when the woods are bare.*

Little Roger noticed an old fallen tree nearby, a tree that was both perpendicular to and a foot off of the ground.

That fallen tree is large enough to support me, he realized. He walked over to the tree and sat down on its fattest section. He then diligently scanned and observed his surroundings some more: the opening of another trail, the batch of pine trees, the meadow in front of him, a small stream to the north, even the large power-line clearing—these were all visible from where he was sitting.

Sit, wait, observe, and be quiet—that's what Mr. Bellefleur told me, he remembered. *Let the deer come to you.*

He sat patiently, hoping to see a deer.

***

Fifteen minutes into his deer hunt, Little Roger thought, *Gosh, my left foot is cold ... details, details, just like Mr. Bellefleur said. Boy, why didn't I inspect the ground near the brook? I would have seen the mud, and then I would have decided to jump over the brook at some other place.*

He quickly scanned his surroundings, and then he decided to pray the following: *Dear Lord, help me see and shoot a deer. Just this one time, Lord, so I can become a man. My parents, my friends—they would all be amazed at my accomplishment. Please, Lord.*

Twenty minutes passed. The sun was quickly setting, and Little Roger started feeling cold. For some unknown reason, he started thinking about the fox.

I would never shoot a fox, Lord. The fox is too beautiful an animal to shoot. That's why one must trap a fox—just like Pépère Long does.

***

Little Roger waited patiently. At one point, he heard a rustling sound to his left, so he quickly turned in the direction of the noise, but he saw nothing. He heard the sound again—like the sound of a small animal walking on fallen leaves. He again looked in the direction of the noise. *Nothing. Hmm?* He scanned the area some more. *Oh, there it is.* It was a small bird, a small robin walking on fallen leaves.

Not even a partridge, he thought. *Just a small little robin can produce all that noise. Hmm? That reminds me ...* He started thinking about something ... something he couldn't quite remember, but ...

Don't look for partridge to fly too often, Little Roger, his brother Bill had once told him when they were hunting together. It was one of Bill's hunting tips to his younger brother, and observing the robin made Little Roger now remember that tip. *Partridges don't fly very well or for very long,* Bill had advised him. *They spend most of their time walking on the ground to* feed. And sometimes, if you're quiet, you can hear partridge when they're walking on leaves.

Little Roger kept looking at the small robin.

Boy, I remember the first time I saw a partridge, he thought. *It was three years ago, and I was hunting with Bill. It was about a mile up the hill, up the trail from here. Me and Bill were walking, and all of a sudden I thought I heard machine-gun fire. My heart started racing. The sound was of a partridge flying maybe four feet from the ground. It's incredible the sound a partridge makes when it flies. It sounds like machine-gun fire.*

Little Roger kept looking at the small robin. Finally it flew away, and when it did Little Roger prayed: *Dear Lord, I really don't want to see any partridge or rabbits—not now, anyway. Now I'm into deer hunting. I just need to kill a deer, Lord. That's all I'm asking.*

He went back to scanning his surroundings, but he saw and heard nothing for ten straight minutes, and then his bottom started getting sore, and his hands were getting cold.

***

More minutes passed. Little Roger thought, *I had some good hunts with Bill. In fact, I still remember the first time I saw Bill shoot a rabbit. It was a day just like today. It was right around this time, too—five P.M. or so. Me and Bill were hunting, but we were heading back home because it was dark and cold out. As we were walking, we both saw a bright white ball about seventy-five feet to our left. Bill knew right away what it was, but I didn't. Bill raised his .410 rifle and prepared himself for a better shot because there were a lot of tree trunks in the way. Then the white ball started running. That's when I realized it was a rabbit. The rabbit started running and hopping fast, and then Bill yelled "Ho!" in a loud voice. I was so surprised because when Bill yelled "Ho!" the bright white rabbit stopped frozen right there, and that's when Bill shot it. Poor rabbit—its bright white fur gave it away. Its color was the opposite of camouflage. I think we had a snowfall in late September that year, and probably all the rabbits' furs turned white. But then the snow melted right away because we had an unusual warm spell. That's why the rabbits were so easy to see in the woods that year. White balls in the brown-gray woods—that's what the rabbits were that season. They were easy-to-spot white balls. I bet plenty of foxes had an easy time spotting those white rabbits when there was no snow on the ground. Dear Lord, I don't want to see rabbits today. I also feel bad the rabbits are sometimes so easy to see in the woods. I'm here to kill a deer, Lord. That's what I have to do to become a man.*

More minutes passed. Little Roger remembered there was something that had bothered him about that particular rabbit hunt ... something ...

What was it that bothered me about that rabbit hunt?

He kept scanning his surroundings while pondering, *What bothered me about that hunt?*

He kept thinking ... He felt his nose getting runny, so he swiped his nose with the top of his left hand. He kept thinking ... and then he blew warm breath into his cupped hands to warm them up.

Yes, yes. Now I remember. Dear Lord, it was very sad to see and hear that rabbit die. Bill had a good shot at it, but the bright white rabbit didn't die right away. It just lay there, motionless, but me and Bill knew it wasn't dead—we knew it was dying but not dead because we could hear the rabbit cry.

Rabbits cry, Lord. I know this because I've seen it and heard it. Rabbits have this fast crying sound to them when they've been shot but they're not dead yet. I remember Bill got closer to that bright white rabbit, and then he took another shot at it—the mercy shot. Then the rabbit stopped crying. I remember Bill picking up the dead rabbit, and I remember I touched the rabbit myself. It was still warm, Lord. I remember asking Bill, "Was that the rabbit making that crying sound?" And he told me, "Yes, Little Roger, rabbits cry when they're suffering." It was tough for me to hear the rabbit cry like that, Lord. Please, Lord, if I see a deer, I want a good clean shot. I don't want to see your beautiful animal suffer.

Little Roger kept scanning his surroundings. He kept quiet while sitting on the fallen tree; he kept listening for any sound; he kept thinking about the many hunting experiences he had with his brother, Bill; and at times he also wondered, *Why didn't I check the brook closer? ... I would have seen the loose mud ... gosh, my left foot is cold.*

***

Ten minutes passed. Little Roger didn't see any animals—not even a robin, and not the beautiful fox he had seen earlier. He looked to his left and noticed how some previously sunlit areas were being replaced by dark shades. It was getting colder, too.

Well, I still have tomorrow morning to hunt, he thought. *And who knows, maybe I'll see a deer on my way back home.*

He stood up and started backtracking his way home by walking at a good clip, and he kept looking out for deer.

Thank you, Lord. Though I didn't accomplish my goal, I did see another one of your beautiful animals—the fox. Thank you, Lord.

In no time, Little Roger had crossed the open meadow and headed down the wooded hill. When he was halfway down the hill, he quickly turned to look up at the wide power-line clearing. He was hoping to see a deer, but he saw no animals so he kept walking.

Up ahead, to the north, Little Roger could see the Desjardin buckwheat farm to his right. The sight of it reminded him of *ployes*, the popular buckwheat flour pancakes many Valley residents regularly ate.

I like ployes *a lot,* thought Little Roger as he continued walking down the hill, *but I prefer bread, especially Mommy's homemade bread.*

He kept walking at a brisk pace.

I still got tomorrow to see and shoot a deer, he reminded himself. *That's the last day I've got to be a man.*

After ten minutes of walking, Little Roger saw Bea Daigle's potato field. To Little Roger's far right, maybe an eighth of a mile away, was a small pond. He caught a glimpse of the pond, and then he stopped walking.

Darn, my hands are cold, he thought as he blew warm breath on his cupped hands. *My cold wet left foot isn't bothering me as much as long as I keep walking, but my hands are getting colder.* He took a good look at the small pond.

That's where me and Eric Desjardin caught that big ten-inch rainbow trout three years ago. Eric finally got the big trout to bite on his hook. I helped out by maneuvering the fish net to haul in our big catch.

Little Roger started replaying the entire fish catch in his mind.

I remember everything, he thought as he continued to blow more warm breath into his cold cupped hands. *I remember me and Eric were so happy to catch that big trout. Poor Eric—that sure was sad when he passed away. He was my best friend at the time.*

It was two years ago that Eric Desjardin, age nine, died of leukemia.

Eric was way more into the outdoors than me. He was great at fishing, and he would have been a great hunter, too. He also was real good at soccer. Poor Eric—I miss him. I remember I was one of the altar boys at his funeral. It was sad.

Little Roger made a sign of the cross as he thought, *Rest in peace, Eric, rest in peace.* He looked at the small pond again, and then he picked up his shotgun and started walking back to his house.

Minutes later, Little Roger came up on Bea Daigle's recently harvested potato field. A steady breeze was blowing from the west.

I better pick up my pace, he thought as he kept walking, *because this breeze makes the temperature colder.* He started taking bigger and faster steps, and in no time he reached the brook that had to be crossed.

Fool me once, shame on you; fool me twice, shame on me. I won't make the same mistake twice—no way Jose—because this time I won't jump where there's any mud.

He took about ten paces to the north, scanned the area carefully, and then he jumped over the narrow brook where he was certain dry grassy earth would serve as his landing zone.

***

Um, nice smell, he thought as he walked up his parents' paved driveway. He consciously slowed his walking pace. *Sure like the smell of freshly cut grass. I see that Dad mowed the front lawn while I was gone hunting. I bet this will be the last time Dad mows the lawn this year because the fall foliage is past and snow can hit us any time now.*

He entered his parents' home, and as soon as he did, he heard his mom say, "Go wash your hands, *Ti Roger.* Dinner's ready. And please remember to leave your boots in the garage."

"Yes, Mom," said Little Roger as he went straight to his bedroom to change his clothes and socks and to unload and safeguard his shotgun.

* * *

"Well, I've got some exciting news," Bob said as Jeannette was serving haddock fish, mashed potatoes, and peas. On Fridays the Nadeaus, like many Catholics, always ate fish. "Little Roger, you should have stayed here this afternoon and not gone hunting."

"Why's that, Dad?" asked Little Roger as he poured himself a glass of milk.

"Because Senator Bill Cohen was walking through town today. I was mowing the front lawn and—Little Roger, pass me both the bread and some of the *ployes* please—thank you. Like I was saying, I was mowing the front lawn and Senator Cohen stopped to talk to me. A couple cars stopped, and people got out to speak to him, too. Nice man, that Cohen. He asked me a lot of questions about trade with Canada and our work at the paper mill. He wanted to know about our union at Fraser Paper, too."

"That's nice, Bob," said Jeannette as she served peas to Little Roger. "I must have just missed Senator Cohen. I had to work a little bit longer today." She paused for a second or two, and then she said, "I sure wish our textile mill was unionized. A lot of our older workers have problems with their hands. They get arthritis a lot. And some weeks the mill only gives us twenty-five hours of work. Overtime for working more than forty hours a week is unheard of—no way will they give us more than forty hours of work per week, because they don't want to pay us time-and-a-half."

"Well, maybe you'll get a union one day, honey," said Bob in an encouraging tone. He took a bite of fish, chewed on it, and then added, "But unions get crazy sometimes, too. At Fraser, if a light bulb goes out, I can't change it because the work rules say we have to call one of the electricians to change a light bulb. And if it's Sunday night at eleven o'clock and there's no electrician on shift, then we have to call an electrician at home, and he'll get paid double time for coming in and changing a light bulb."

The Nadeaus kept eating quietly. At one point, Little Roger asked, "Mommy, can I have *cretons* with my *ployes*?" referring to the pork-meat spread popular in French Canadian cuisine.

"*Non, mon Ti Roger.* No *cretons* on Friday—remember, no meat on Fridays," she said.

Little Roger sighed. "Yes, Mommy—no meat on Fridays." He quickly changed the topic and asked, "Daddy, was Senator Cohen the same politician we saw two years ago in Fort Kent? We went out for hot dogs at Rocks and there was a politician there. Was that the same man?"

"Yes, Little Roger," Bob said. "You have a good memory."

"And what party is Senator Cohen, Daddy?"

"He's a Republican," said Bob as he buttered a *ploye*.

"Republicans don't like unions, Bob," Jeannette interjected. "If and when I become an American citizen, I will vote for the Democrats."

"Oh, that's not always true, honey," Bob retorted. "Not all Republicans hate unions. Plus, Cohen's Jewish. He sometimes votes with the Democrats, so I bet he doesn't hate unions, because the Democrats love unions. And Little Roger, don't ever agree with the people who talk bad about the only Jewish family in the Valley, the Kramers in Fort Kent."

"Okay, Daddy," said Little Roger. He took a sip of milk.

"Jews, like Senator Cohen, are very hard workers," Bob said. "Some people talk bad about the Kramers, but Mr. Kramer worked very hard at starting and running his car and truck dealership. Some people talk bad about Mr. Kramer because they are jealous of rich people. Don't be jealous of what others have, Little Roger."

"Yes, Daddy," responded Little Roger. He made a mental note to put that tidbit in his Valley history paper: *The Valley, at least on the American side, only has one Jewish family.*

Bob continued, "And take the multi-millionaire potato-farmer J.R. Simplot, Little Roger. He's the big man from Idaho."

"Yes, Daddy, I remember what you said last year about Mr. Simplot."

"That's right, Little Roger," said Bob. "It was last year's potato season when Mr. Simplot visited the Valley. I remember the local farmers here met Mr. Simplot in Fort Kent. Bea Daigle told me he shook Mr. Simplot's hand. He also told me Mr. Simplot was planning on buying potato farms both in Maine and in New Brunswick, Canada. Did you know Mr. Simplot is a big supplier for McDonald's french fries, Little Roger?"

"Yes, Daddy, I remember you told me that last year. I love McDonald's french fries."

"I do too, Little Roger. Everybody likes McDonald's french fries. And the point is, Little Roger, that Mr. Simplot is very rich, but again, we shouldn't be jealous of him. Heck, Bea Daigle told me Mr. Simplot had a driver driving him around the Valley last year. Drove around in a big white Lincoln. And I've heard more than once that during Mr. Simplot's visit last year, Mr. Simplot would tell his driver to stop at a house every thirty minutes or so."

"Why's that, Daddy?" asked Little Roger.

"Because Mr. Simplot was busy playing the mercantile—the stock market for commodities. You see, Little Roger, that's how Mr. Simplot makes some of his money—he plays the mercantile. Of course, he also makes a lot of money selling potatoes to McDonald's for all those french fries, but he also plays the mercantile, and Mr. Simplot had to make phone calls every thirty minutes or so to tell his broker to buy or sell. That's why during Mr. Simplot's visit to the Valley last year, he would tell his driver to stop at someone's house—any house—and ask the homeowner if he could use the phone to make a commodity trade."

"So Mr. Simplot is a trader, Daddy?"

"Yes, Little Roger, a commodity trader and a big potato farmer. And Mr. Simplot made sure he paid the homeowner for their phone use as well. Bea Daigle told me every time Mr. Simplot made a phone call, he would give a twenty-dollar bill to the homeowner for the phone use, even if the call took just a minute or so."

"Are you sure about that, Bob?" Jeannette chimed in. "Paying twenty dollars for a quick phone call. My, that Mr. Simplot must be really rich."

"Yes, dear, he is," said Bob. "Pass me another *ploye*, Little Roger. Yes, Mr. Simplot is very rich, and that's the whole point, Little Roger—don't be jealous of others, and don't be jealous of rich people. Most rich people like Mr. Kramer and Mr. Simplot worked very hard to establish their businesses. Don't be jealous of others, Little Roger."

The dinner conversation shifted to Jeannette planning to organize a potluck dinner for Josephine Dube because "her thirty-two-year-old-daughter in Hartford, Connecticut, recently died of cervical cancer ... As you know, Bob, we don't make much money at the textile mill, and Josephine's husband recently got laid off at the sawmill."

"Sure, honey," responded Bob. "A potluck dinner for the Dube's would be nice. I'll see what the Knights of Columbus can do, too. Ed Dube's a good man—I'm sorry to hear he got laid off."

After dinner, Little Roger went to his bedroom to read. Reading about something that interested him—fun reading— was what Little Roger often did after dinner, and on that particular Friday evening Little Roger read a portion of a book about the history of the Boston Red Sox. After just five minutes of reading, Little Roger was of the opinion that *we should have never sold Babe Ruth's contract to the New York Yankees. The Curse of the Bambino—that's what it's called. Anyway, looks like the Pirates may come back and win it all this year. My beloved Red Sox winning the World Series—who knows, maybe next year.*

After thirty minutes of reading about Fenway Park, the Curse of the Bambino, Ted Williams, and modern-day players like Jim Rice and Fred Lynn, Little Roger forced himself to read his *O Pioneers!* assignment. He finished that assignment in forty minutes, after which he embarked on his evening regimen of thirty push-ups, thirty sit-ups, and one hundred swings with his weighted baseball bat.

Okay, he thought as he completed his last sit-up. The push-ups had taken just a few minutes to complete, and the sit-ups had also been done quickly. *Now it's time for one hundred swings with the weighted bat, and then I'll go to bed.*

He reached inside his bedroom closet and picked up his old wooden bat, the wooden bat he always placed the donut weight on. He situated himself in a comfortable hitting stance next to his bed, and then he started his one hundred swings.

You can make yourself into a better ballplayer, he reminded himself as he did his swings. At times he would glance at both his Johnny Bench and Pete Rose posters.

That Pete Rose, the great Charlie Hustle. That's the way to play baseball, he thought as he glanced at the poster of the Cincinnati Reds infielder. He continued swinging the weighted bat. *Shoulder to shoulder. Just like Coach Winkin said at the baseball camp.*

Forty-eight. Forty-nine ... Dear Lord, tomorrow's the big day—sorta like game day for sports. It's my last day to kill a deer. Please help me, Lord. I promise to be a good boy.

When he was done with his swings, Little Roger showered, changed into his pajamas, and went to bed.

***

Little Roger had a hard time falling asleep that night, but once he did he soon began to dream about ...

... his dad drinking a beer with Ernest Hemingway in Key West, Florida; seeing the huge bull moose Mr. Voisine had killed last year—the moose was hanging from a big red wrecker crane; hitting a game-winning homerun on a three-two pitch in the bottom of the last inning to win the Valley Little League Championship for Frenchville; remembering how good Emily Levesque looked ... boy, I got a crush on her; I want to get an A on my history paper in Mr. Morneau's class; J.R. Simplot of Idaho driving around the Valley in a big white Lincoln, stopping every thirty minutes to borrow a phone to place mercantile trades and paying twenty bucks each time for the use of the phone; images of the beautiful red fox from earlier that day; a white rabbit crying and suffering; killing a big buck deer and thus becoming a man ...

In the middle of the night, Little Roger suddenly awoke in a cold sweat. His heart was racing, and he realized that he had been dreaming ... but of what? The only thing he could remember about his latest dream was seeing Mr. Voisine's dead bull moose hanging from a large tow-truck crane. *But in the dream the moose is still alive and his eyes are wide open and looking at me,* Little Roger remembered.

What Little Roger couldn't remember were all the other parts of his dreams, including ... *seeing* Pépère *Long trapping the beautiful fox from that afternoon; the beautiful fox struggling to get out of the trap; seeing* Pépère *Long approaching quickly to club the fox to death; running up to the fox and attempting to free it.*

"*Now* Ti Roger, *leave that trap alone," says* Pépère *Long in French. "That fox fur will be worth a lot of money."*

"*Non non,* Pépère" *yells Little Roger, hurrying and struggling to free the fox. "Let this one fox go,* Pépère."

"Non, mon Ti Roger," *says* Pépère *Long.*

And then Little Roger successfully frees the fox, but he immediately hears his dad, who's up on a nearby hill, say, "Little Roger, you shouldn't have done that." Little Roger looks up and sees Ernest Hemingway standing next to his dad. Both Hemingway and Dad are drinking beer, and then the next thing Little Roger notices is Pépère *Long running past him, not with a club but with a rifle.* Pépère *Long suddenly stops running, aims his rifle, and shoots the fox, killing it instantly.*

Then Little Roger's dream shifts, this time to him walking by the large tow-truck crane, the large tow-truck crane with the bull moose hanging from it. Though the moose has been killed for some time, Little Roger notices that as he passes the crane and the moose hanging from it, the moose's eyes are still open—eyes that seem to be full of life and peering directly at Little Roger and ...

Little Roger woke up in a cold sweat. He knew he had been dreaming, *but of what?* He was thirsty so he got up, went to the kitchen, and got himself a glass of water. He then went back to bed. Once asleep, he started dreaming again.

***

Little Roger woke up at six-fifteen the next morning. It was a Saturday, and it was the last day Little Roger had to achieve his goal of killing a deer and becoming a man.

He fixed himself a breakfast consisting of a bowl of Corn Flakes, a glass of orange juice, and two pieces of toast with plenty of peanut butter spread on them.

He brushed his teeth after breakfast, and then he put on the same hunting clothes he'd worn less than twenty-four hours before, with two exceptions: this time he added a small pair of brown working gloves to his attire, and he wore thick wool socks instead of the thin pair of white athletic socks he'd worn yesterday.

Don't want cold hands like yesterday, he thought as he placed the brown gloves in one of his back jean pockets. He then grabbed his shotgun and six slugs.

I'm gonna hunt exactly where I did yesterday, he told himself as he left his parents' home. He glanced at his watch. The time was 6:50 A.M. *Hunt alone, be quiet, and pick a good hunting spot. That's what Mr. Bellefleur told me during the ride to school. That spot I had yesterday is as good as any. I just hope I get better luck this morning.*

He walked the exact same path he had the day before—the same path to the same pre-selected hunting spot. This time around, however, he wasn't in a rush because he figured he had five hours of hunting instead of yesterday's ninety minutes or so. And he also didn't leap over the narrow brook in the same spot as yesterday.

Won't make that mistake again, he told himself as he came up on the brook. He walked a bit further south, a place where the brook was even narrower and importantly free of mud, and he jumped over the brook. In no time, he came upon Bea Daigle's recently harvested potato field.

Boy, just a couple weeks ago I was picking potatoes for Mr. Charette in a field just like this one. He started walking through the soft earth of the harvested field. *Had my best day, too, forty-seven barrels. It was the most barrels I ever picked because Mr. Charette's field was russet potatoes, and russet potatoes are big, and so the barrels are easier to fill up.*

He quickly started doing the math as he kept walking.

Hmm, let's see ... I earn thirty-five cents per barrel. Let's say thirty-three cents to make the math easier ... so three barrels makes a dollar. Divide forty-seven by three ... let's say forty-five by three which is fifteen, so I made fifteen bucks that day. Mommy puts all my potato-picking money in a bank account— she does that every fall—and I've been picking potatoes now for ... let's see ... I started at eight, so that's three, no, four years. Mommy always tells me she's saving my potato-picking money so I can buy something later, when I turn seventeen. I know that's how Bill bought the old pickup when he turned seventeen—he used his potato-picking money. Me, I want a new catcher's mitt and some other stuff like ... like ... I don't know, maybe clothes, or maybe I'll buy an old pickup truck like Bill did. That reminds me—Dear Lord, please help Bill in Panama.

Little Roger kept walking through the field. *Sure glad it's not too cold out this morning. It's chilly out, but not too cold— definitely not cold enough for me to wear gloves. Plus, if I wear gloves I won't feel my shotgun trigger as well as I want to. I'll just use the gloves in case it gets colder.*

He kept walking slowly, more slowly than yesterday because he had more hunting time now. In five minutes, he saw the Desjardin Farm out in the distance to his left, and immediately memories of fishing with Eric Desjardin flashed in his mind as he saw the pond again, *the pond where Eric and me caught that big trout.* Little Roger noticed a thick layer of fog above the pond.

Rest in peace, Eric, he thought as he kept walking. *Rest in peace.* He did a quick sign of the cross and kept walking slowly.

***

Ten minutes later, Little Roger was walking uphill. The meadow, the tree line, the trail opening, the pine trees, the small stream, the power lines—these were all in his sights.

Won't be long now, he thought as he trudged uphill. *Today's like game seven of the World Series—there's no tomorrow. I either become a man today or try again next year.* He kept walking uphill, and in no time he came upon the spot where the fox had been resting yesterday.

Good, he thought. *You're a beautiful animal, Mr. Fox, but you'd probably distract deer. It's good you're not in the area this morning, because ...*

Suddenly, out of nowhere, Little Roger heard a horn sound directly above him. He immediately stopped walking and quickly looked up.

Canadian geese, he realized as he saw what was flying above him. *That's their call sign, their horn sign. Thank you, God—thank you for letting me see your beautiful flock of geese this morning. Canadian geese are smart. When it starts getting cold, they head south in that beautiful V-shape pattern of theirs.*

Little Roger resumed walking slowly. He paid particular attention to the power-line clearing because he could clearly see the long distances it covered.

Hmm, he thought. *No deer feeding in the power-line clearing this morning.* He kept walking slowly, and soon his hunting spot came into sight.

There it is, Lord—my hunting spot. Once again, I'll sit on that fallen tree. Today's the day.

He walked in the direction of the fallen tree. He walked slowly and quietly, and when he reached the fallen tree he noticed a small dead branch covering the spot he had sat at some fifteen hours earlier.

Must have been windy up here last night—that's what probably caused this branch to land on the fallen tree. He placed the branch on the ground, then he scanned his surroundings: the trail and batch of pine trees in front of him; the power line clearing to his left; the open meadow slightly to his right; the small stream further to the north in front of him.

Today's the day, Lord. Please help me.

He turned, sat down on the fallen tree, got himself comfortable, and started scanning his surroundings in the hopes of seeing a deer.

***

Eight A.M. passed. Then 8:30, and then 9:15. Little Roger would periodically check the time on his Timex watch wrapped around his left wrist.

I still have plenty of time, but noon's probably my time limit because I've got that football game this afternoon. I've got less than three hours left. Please, Lord, let me see one of your deer.

He kept scanning his surroundings. Ten A.M. passed. He started daydreaming about ...

Pépère Long shooting and killing a caribou; Mr. Voisine posing next to the huge bull moose he killed last year; Pépère

Long trapping a big castor—a big beaver. What an amazing animal the beaver is. He peered at his watch. The time was 10:15. *The fox might be the most beautiful animal out there, but I still think the beaver is the most amazing animal—certainly the hardest working with all those dams they build.*

Soon 10:20 passed, as did 10:30, and 10:45.

Boy, it takes discipline to stay quiet to hunt deer. I sure prefer hunting partridge because at least then I'm walking in the woods. This remain-silent stuff ain't easy. Plus, my butt is starting to hurt.

A thought suddenly hit him.

It ain't cold out, and my gloves in my left back pocket are bothering me—they're creating a hump that's hurting my butt because I'm sitting on them.

He figured he could remove the gloves in his left back pocket with his right hand.

I want to keep holding my shotgun with my left hand because my right hand is my trigger hand.

He reached down and across with his right hand and quickly tugged at his gloves as he ... *oh no ... no ... I'm, I'm ...* he felt himself slowly falling backward ... *I'm losing my balance ...*

He bent down in the hopes of swinging forward to counter the backward falling but he ... *oh no ... I'm ... I'm falling ...*

He landed straight on his back, his shotgun still held up high above him by his left hand.

Crap—what a deer hunter I turned out to be. Can't even sit still on a fallen tree without falling on my back. Any deer out there heard me falling.

Little Roger stood up, dusted himself off, grabbed his gloves from his left back pocket, and placed them in his front left pocket. He then sat down again on the fallen tree.

Now I'll never see any deer.

At 10:50 A.M., Little Roger decided to sit facing the other way—to the south, looking toward the power-line clearing.

What the heck, he thought. *Maybe a change of scenery will be good for me.*

He quietly spun himself around to face south, and as soon as he did he saw a break in the clouds: to his left the sky was gray and foggy, but directly ahead of him he noticed white puffy clouds and small breaks of bright blue sky.

Gonna be a nice afternoon for football. Boy, I sure hope I see a deer in the next hour.

He waited as 11:00 A.M. passed, then 11:15 and 11:20.

Boy, I haven't seen anything except for those nice Canadian geese this morning. Well, at least I'm not cold today. I could urinate, but I'll hold it in. I've got about forty minutes left here.

Suddenly, a short gust of wind blew in from the west heading east. With this gust of wind came the smell of pine trees.

Gosh, pine trees sure smell good, he thought. *Maybe I won't kill a deer today—maybe never. But what's nice is the scenery. The woods, the scenery, the smells—these are all nice things. Thank you, Lord.*

He kept quiet and attentive, and he kept looking at the power-line clearing for deer but saw none. Another five minutes passed, then he decided to spin himself around the fallen tree and face north again like he had for most of the morning.

Maybe my chances will be better if I face north again.

He spun himself around and started scanning the surroundings in front of him, beginning on his left and working toward his right. The batch of pine trees were in front of him but slightly to his left; straight ahead were woods, a mixture of fir trees, spruce trees, and some birch trees; and slightly to his right was the meadow and ...

I see a deer! I see a deer! He was looking at the tree line next to the meadow.

It's a doe—not a buck, but a good-size doe. A doe deer!

His heart started pounding—he could actually feel and hear his heart beating inside him. A quick thought flashed in his mind. It was the thought of his first time hearing a partridge fly, the sound of a rhythmic *tat-tat-tat-tat-tat* like machine-gun fire. That was three years ago when he had first heard a partridge fly. The sound had scared him and made his heart race then, and now his heart was racing and thumping again, *thump, thump, thump.*

Dear God—a deer about sixty yards from me!

He tried to compose himself, even though tons of thoughts ran through his mind:

The doe is too far for me to shoot at.

It's a big doe.

Gosh, what a beautiful animal it is, the deer. Very well-designed.

The doe is hardly moving. It's just there, right on the edge of the tree line and the meadow, and it's not moving.

The doe is light brown.

Thank you, Lord, thank you for this opportunity.

Stay quiet!

A few seconds passed. Little Roger took a deep breath and felt himself becoming calmer. He couldn't feel that thumping sound in his chest anymore, so that was good. He kept his eyes on the doe. The doe had its head down and was feeding. It hardly moved.

She probably won't just run away on me, he thought. *At least not if she's feeding.*

He kept his eyes zeroed in on the deer. The doe's head and eyes faced to the east—away from Little Roger.

I'm guessing the doe's sixty yards from me. Sixty yards to the northeast—that's too far to shoot at. He remembered Mr. Bellefleur's advice on the topic. *I need to shoot from thirty yards out. Plus, the best place to shoot a deer is in the shoulder, and I don't have a good shoulder shot.*

The doe kept feeding—its head was right next to the ground. Little Roger was surprisingly calm. Like the doe, he too hardly moved at all.

Well, the doe's too far, he thought, *so I better get closer to her or hope she comes to me.*

Just then, the doe took three steps forward.

Deer, you're moving in the wrong direction. Come the other way.

The doe took another three steps.

You're moving in the wrong direction again, Mrs. Doe. I'll never be a man if you keep moving away from me.

The doe's head went down in the grasses to feed.

If I stand up that probably won't make any noise, he figured. *What the heck—I'll stand up.*

Little Roger slowly and quietly stood up. He kept his eyes fixed on the doe. Nothing changed—the doe was still feeding and stationary.

The deer is way too far to shoot at, but there are very few leaves in front of me. Maybe I can walk quietly in the direction of the beautiful doe, and I won't make noise because I won't be stepping on leaves.

While pointing his shotgun at the doe, Little Roger took a step forward, a step with his left leg. The doe didn't move. He then took another step forward, this time with his right leg. Same result—no movement by the doe.

Maybe this is what I need to do—walk closer to the deer and get a good shot.

Little Roger stood motionless for around fifteen seconds, then he took another two steps forward. The doe didn't move. He took another two steps forward, and again the doe didn't move. He felt his heart beating faster.

I'll stay here for a while. If the deer doesn't move, then I'll try getting closer again.

He kept staring at the doe.

It's a beautiful animal—deer are beautiful animals, and just as he thought that, the doe started walking in a northwesterly direction—not directly in Little Roger's direction, but a bit closer to him and, importantly, in a direction that gave Little Roger a better view and a better shot.

He felt his heart beating even faster. *Good deer, good doe. Keep moving, Ms. Doe, keep moving in that direction.*

The doe suddenly stopped trotting. Little Roger figured the doe was maybe fifty yards from him. He quickly considered the shot he had.

Some small trees and branches, but not a bad shot, he figured. *But the problem is distance.*

He slowly took a step forward to close the distance gap. He again felt his heart beating faster. The doe didn't move.

Okay, okay, he thought. *Stay calm. Maybe I can get closer.*

He started to take a step forward and ...

Dear Lord! Dear Lord! The doe is coming this way!

Little Roger's heart was thumping inside his chest again. He aimed his shotgun at the doe.

C'mon deer, c'mon Ms. Doe. Get closer now.

The doe suddenly stopped. Little Roger's eyes blinked rapidly. He tried to calm down, but he was having a hard time doing that. He felt his hands trembling—not a lot, just a slight trembling.

He took a deep breath.

This is a pretty good shot, but I'm still too far away. I need to close the gap by another twenty yards.

Twenty yards—that was the distance gap.

I might scare the doe away if I get any closer. And deer can really move fast. I remember I saw deer on television jump over tall fences and hop around in ways that make them impossible to shoot.

He kept staring at the doe, and in the process he caught a glimpse of the doe's eyes.

He slowly and quietly took a step forward. A few seconds passed, and then the doe surprisingly moved closer to him by some ten yards. Little Roger quickly decided to take another step forward. He did, and the doe didn't move.

The doe's about thirty yards away now. If only the doe could turn and not face me directly, I'd have the best shot.

More seconds passed. Little Roger started thinking fast:

Take a shot now?

Hope deer turns so I can have a shoulder shot?

Wait some more?

Take a few more steps? No. Distance wasn't an issue anymore. Plus, he again feared the doe would scoot away if he got too close.

He decided to wait some more. Some ten seconds passed, then the doe raised her head, but she didn't turn. After a few seconds, the doe's head and neck returned to the grasses to feed.

Little Roger waited, and then ...

Gosh darnit—is my shotgun loaded? He felt his heart pound.

He held his shotgun with his right hand, and with his left hand he reached for the left-side pocket of his orange hunter's jacket.

I feel three slugs—that's what I figured, but my right-side pocket better have two slugs. I know I placed three slugs in the left pocket and three slugs in the right pocket this morning. Did I load my shotgun when I crossed U.S. Route 1? Better have two slugs in my right pocket, which would mean the other slug's loaded in my shotgun.

While still looking at the doe, Little Roger slowly moved his left hand to hold his shotgun, and with his right hand he reached into his jacket's right-hand pocket.

Boy, I hope I feel two slugs, he thought. *Two and not three. If I feel three, then I know my gun's not loaded.*

His hand and fingers felt around the pocket.

Whew—I feel two slugs. Yes, yes, it's two slugs. It's definitely two slugs. Thank you, God. That means I did load my shotgun this morning. He decided to double check, though.

It won't make too much noise if I crack open my shotgun and look at the barrel.

Quietly and diligently, Little Roger placed his weapon on safe by moving the safety lever down.

Good, he thought. *Weapon's on safe.* He slowly cracked-open his 16-gauge shotgun, and there he saw a slug occupying the barrel.

Okay, whew. He slowly snapped the barrel back in position, all while keeping his eyes on the doe. The doe didn't move.

I don't have the shoulder shot, though. He waited quietly, all while pointing his shotgun at the doe.

Seconds passed. The doe kept feeding. More seconds passed. *C'mon doe, turn so I can have a shoulder shot.* More seconds passed. Then suddenly the doe did turn slightly toward Little Roger, and that's when he instinctively lined up the BB-sight at the end of his shotgun's barrel with the doe's shoulder.

Darnit! he thought as he realized his shotgun was still on safe. *This ain't a big problem though. All I have to do is move the safety lever to the fire position.*

He placed his right thumb on the safety lever and slowly guided the lever to the off-safety position. A very short click sound resulted from this, but it was barely audible, and he noticed the doe hadn't moved at all even after the click sound.

This is as good of a shot as I'll get.

He delicately maneuvered his right index finger to the trigger. He felt his left hand tremble a bit, but his trigger finger and trigger hand—his right hand—were steady.

Stay calm, he thought, *and don't let your hand tremble … won't be long now.*

He took a steady aim at the doe's shoulder, and that's when the doe's head spun to the left. The doe was looking directly at Little Roger and the opposite was true too, for Little Roger was now looking directly at the doe's head, face, and eyes.

Seconds passed, and then … then … then Little Roger slowly guided his shotgun down. He was staring at the doe, the doe was staring at him. Neither he nor the doe moved—they just stared at each other, their eyes fixated on one another.

Go away, deer, go away, he thought as he slowly took his finger off the trigger. He still kept staring at the doe, and the doe just stared back.

Little Roger took a step forward. The doe didn't move. He took another step—same result. But then, after Little Roger took a third step forward, the doe dashed away, but only for twenty feet or so. Little Roger took a few more steps toward the doe, and the doe eventually trotted away further.

Little Roger was calm. He started walking toward the trail and open meadow. He looked to his left to see if the doe was still in sight. She was, but barely. He quickly looked at his watch.

The time was 12:05. He placed his shotgun on safe and resumed walking down the trail.

***

After just a minute or two of walking, Little Roger stopped, turned around, and looked to see if the doe was still in sight. She wasn't.

I couldn't do it, Lord—not today, he told God as he resumed walking down the trail. *You know what it was, Lord? It was the beauty of the animal—that's what bothered me. That doe's eyes were looking directly at me, Lord. Those doe eyes ... there was something about those eyes, Lord.* Little Roger thought hard, but he couldn't seem to put his finger on it ... *something about those eyes ... as if the doe was saying "Who are you and why are you about to shoot me?" Lord, it was as if I had seen those eyes before. Those eyes had stared at me before, Lord. Where have I seen those eyes?*

Frustrated, he shrugged the thought off and kept walking down the trail.

***

When he reached his parents' house, Little Roger quickly unloaded his shotgun and placed it under his bed. After that, he went to the bathroom to urinate, and then he went to his bedroom to change into some workout clothes—sweatpants and a sweatshirt. While changing clothes in his bedroom, he thought:

My 16-gauge didn't fail me today—that would be like blaming your bat for looking at strike three pass you by. You can't blame your bat if you don't swing at pitches, and I can't blame my shotgun today because I didn't pull the trigger.

He finished changing his clothes, and then he stepped inside the kitchen.

"How was the hunting, *Ti* Roger?" asked his mother. She was busy cleaning a countertop.

"Oh, okay Mom," said Little Roger, not really sure what to say.

"Did you see anything? Any partridge out there?"

He started thinking fast. He quickly decided the easy thing was to say he saw nothing. That's what he really wanted to tell his mom because he wasn't in the mood to talk about seeing a deer—admitting he saw a deer would bring out tons of questions and comments like, *How big was the deer? Was it a buck? If it's a buck, how many points did it have? Remember how I told you that growing up in Clair, a boy is only considered a man once he kills a deer?*

"Uh, no, Mom, I didn't see anything this morning—not even a partridge," Little Roger said, lying. Right then he promised God, *I'll confess this sin of lying at Mass tonight, Lord. Just a little white lie. I'll confess it*

"Well, your father's gone to pick up Lisa in St. Agatha," said his mom as Little Roger was walking toward the kitchen sink to get a glass of water. "Lisa told us she had a good time in Quebec City."

"That's nice," said Little Roger. He was placing a glass under the tap.

"Are you hungry, dear?" asked his Mom. "I can make you a sandwich."

"Sure, Mom," said Little Roger. He was hungry.

"What type of sandwich do you want?"

"Oh, whatever's easier for you, Mom."

"How about a BLT?"

"Sounds great," said Little Roger. He proceeded to drink the glass of water.

"And do you want a side of fiddleheads with that? I still have some leftover frozen fiddleheads from this past spring. Remember when Lisa and I picked all those fiddleheads near the St. John River?"

"Yes, Mommy, I remember," said Little Roger. He especially liked the tender little rolls of fern with melted butter and a touch of pepper. "And yes, I'll have some fiddleheads with my BLT sandwich. Oh and Mom, I'll be outside playing toss. I'll be back in ten minutes—promise."

"Okay, fine," said his mother, "but make sure you wash your hands before eating your sandwich."

"Okay, Mom."

Little Roger went back to his bedroom to get his catcher's mitt and a tennis ball. When he played toss—throwing the tennis ball against one of the sidewalls of his parents' home—Little Roger always used an old soft tennis ball. He quickly got his black Cooper's catcher's mitt and an old tennis ball. He then laced up his sneakers and headed outside.

He started throwing the tennis ball on the eastern side of his parents' home. While doing so, various thoughts ran through his mind:

Pépère *Long hunting and trapping.*

Mr. Bellefleur's advice on hunting deer.

The beautiful fox I saw yesterday.

The nice doe I saw this morning.

The football game this afternoon that kicks off in about an hour.

My brother Bill is missing. Please Lord, help us find Bill.

Little Roger kept throwing the tennis ball off the sidewall. More thoughts came to him, thoughts of the Pirates staging a comeback against the Orioles; his history paper for Mr. Morneau's class; who his teammates would be for next year's Little League team.

And then ...

Where I'm from, in Clair, New Brunswick, a boy is not considered a man until he kills a deer.

They were the words his mother had told him just two days ago.

To be a man you have to kill a deer, he thought. He kept throwing and catching the tennis ball.

***

"*Ti* Roger, your BLT sandwich is ready," he heard his mother say minutes later. He turned around to find his mom standing next to the garage door some eighty feet from him.

"Okay Mom, I'll be right in."

"And be sure to wash your hands," his mom reminded him as she headed back inside the house.

Little Roger tucked the tennis ball inside his catcher's mitt, and then he turned slightly to his right and looked at the St. John River. Behind the dark and slow-flowing river he saw a few homes, and beyond those few homes Little Roger noticed the steep wooded hills of the Valley.

The hills are mostly gray now because the hardwoods are naked, leafless, he thought. *Of course there's the patches of green here and there—those are the patches of fir trees and pine trees.* The thought of green patches of pine trees reminded him of his deer-hunting spot.

He started walking toward the garage, and as he did he felt a cool wind wisp by.

Fall doesn't last long in the Valley—soon winter will set in He looked up at the sky.

The sun is trying to break through those darkish gray clouds. Well, at least it's still decent weather for football. And then he thought: *To be a man you have to kill a deer. Not now Lord, not now. Who knows—maybe next year.*

THE END

About the Author

Paul Bouchard is the author of *Enlistment, A Package at Gitmo,* and the nonfiction book *A Catholic Marries a Hindu.* He grew up in northern Maine and is currently a lawyer in the Army JAG Corps. For more on Paul Bouchard visit www.authorpaulbouchard.com.